Table of Contents

by Phyllis A. Collmann

ISBN: 979-8-218-62993-9

For additional copies of this or other books
written by Phyllis A. Collmann:
www.collmannwarehouse.com (website)
www.phylliscollmann.com (blog)
phyllisacollmann@hotmail.com (email)
1-712-552-2030 (phone)

Phyllis A. Collmann
22698 C12, Ireton, IA 51027-8016

Printed in the United States of America

Dedication

To my husband of 72 years, who is now deceased
To my children: Cynthia, Kimberly, Ronald and Melonie
To all my grandchildren & great-grandchildren

Special Thank You To...

Julie Ann Madden for typing and editing.

Diane Ten Napel and Colleen Westergard-Baker for all your kindness and support as I've begun my new journey.

Cynthia Wurr, Kimberly Ann Bonnett, Ronald Collmann, & Melonie Collmann Luban for all your love and support

.

FEARED FOR MY LIFE

by Phyllis A. Collmann

Chapter 1

These events are based on a true story written by me, Margaret Dolon. If you are lucky to live a long time. Me, I have. Things you see may surprise you, even shock you. You try to remain calm and remember nothing you're seeing pertains to you or concerns you until it suddenly does.

After a person faces a heart-wrenching situation in life, everything changes. You hurt in every part of your mind and body. You feel alone and defeated.

Your home life is not ever the same. You feel you need to make some changes but you have no idea what to change. You can move furniture or you can paint a few rooms.

In your stress, you remember you have to eat. You have to pay bills. Your mail is still coming. Eating requires going to the grocery store for food. You have to get out of the house and into the outside world eventually.

First, in order to understand, you have to live through a terrible heartache. After a few months, your body begins to fight back. You begin to have pain and discomfort in places in your body you had never experienced before.

All the home remedies you had always had cures from did not help at all. If you are an active person, staying in bed later in the morning or elevating your sore leg can only last a short time.

While your heart is aching, your body hurts in a new area and, of course, your brain is working overtime.

Remembering is the ongoing problem. Try telling your brain to think of something different.

Try remembering the day of the week it is or the date of the week it is. Time slips away from you overnight.

So, when you have a pain that just keeps hurting, you find it unbearable. Asking for help is your only hope.

Chapter 2

When you are now living in a new area with your family, you depend on their choice of help. An appointment to a nearby facility is best. From there you are sent to a larger, more knowledgeable hospital facility.

My sister, Jill, sister Ruth, and brothers Ben and Larry, made a call and an appointment was marked on the calendar.

The doctor examined the area of pain and decided more care than he could give was needed. So, another appointment was made and a short drive across town was ordered.

It was not a surprise when arriving to find the very

large waiting room was full. The nurses were working very hard to take care of every person's pain, injury and sickness. Masks were handed out, trying to stop any disease from spreading.

A special machine was ordered for my pain and knee part. The machine was located in the back of the building, down several different halls. I was directed to ride in a wheelchair because of the distance from the main part of the facility.

Chapter 3

After arriving at the room I was asked to lay down on a paper-covered bed. I was put in an upright position. I could look down a long hall. At the end of the hall I could see a man in a wheelchair accompanied by several policemen.

He looked straight at me. His eyes looked directly at me. I was curious as I looked back at him.

Then I could see he had handcuffs on with a chain going down fro his handcuffs to a a chain around each of his ankles. He had no shoes on. He wore a T-shirt and shorts. His eyes still looked directly at me. There was nothing else to look at but each other. My body was cold waiting for the procedure but not as cold as his eyes. He continued to stare directly at me.

I looked at the ceiling, then the walls. Then turned

and looked back and his eyes had never left my face.

He suddenly leaned over and from the distance I felt he was crying in discomfort. A nurse approached him and took care of his problem. He sat back up and looked right at me.

One hour passed, and he never took his eyes off of me.

I had the procedure and then another long wait for the results to be read.

A kind nurse brought me a warm blanket. My cold body was screaming for the blanket. I felt then I could get through this waiting for the next doctor's diagnosis order.

After that, I had to wait for medicine from the pharmacy.

One hour-and-forty-five minutes later with his eyes still looking directly at me, I was told I could leave. The worst part was, in order to leave the building, I had to walk down the hall toward him. Walk right next to his wheelchair. The fear was mounting more each minute.

I tried to keep my eyes looking at the floor while I walked by him. It was most difficult as I knew he was staring at me. My nerves were on edge. My body was cold and shaking as I walked by his wheelchair.

I got to the door and pushed against it to get it opened. The warm air was so welcome on my body. I needed to warm up and get the picture of him staring at me out of my mind.

Chapter 4

Getting into my car and driving to my new home was a great relief. I went into the house, closed the door, locked it, and pulled all the drapes closed. I turned only one small light on. Eating did not interest me, only getting some rest and getting the man's face out of my head.

The shower I took was fast and extra warm. I crawled into my bed and immediately went to sleep. At 2 a.m., I was wide awake, thinking I heard a noise in the house. The first vision I saw was the man's face, looking directly at me. My heart was pounding so hard and fast. I knew if I didn't calm down I'd have a heart attack. I laid my head back on my pillow and covered up. I laid in the dark, and a thought came into my mind. What if the man asked someone who I was and, worst of all, where I lived?

I couldn't leave now or move. My family was caring for me.

Morning finally came after lying awake for hours. I did not leave the house for a couple of days.

The night before my next appointment, as a follow-up, I had another nightmare. Hearing a tapping on my bedroom window, I sat straight up in bed with the man's face at the end of my bed. I slipped out of bed and as quietly as I could, checked each window.

No one was there. I had imagined hearing the noise. I finished the night staring at the ceiling.

I dressed for my appointment and then drove across town, feeling tired and lonely. I had not confided in my family about the man in the wheelchair or all the sleepless nights. But, I was sure I could not go on like this.

I parked my car a short distance from the entrance to the doctor's door. As I crawled out of my car, I looked at the distance I had to walk.

I looked and the man leaving the doctor's office was the man I had seen in the wheelchair. My first reaction was to get back in my car and go to my house. He turned his head and looked right at me.

My body began to shiver and I was extremely cold. My heart was racing. He took a couple steps toward me, then turned; pulled back by two policemen, one on each side of him.

My mind stopped working. I stood in a cold meltdown, not knowing what to do or how to move. He was nowhere in sight now. I suddenly realized if I was in the building, I would be safer than standing in an open parking lot.

In minutes, I was in the waiting room. I registered, then sat down nearest the desk, thinking I would be safe there. Seeing the doctor took only a short period of time. I got to the door, stepped out and looked in every direction. No one was in the parking lot. No police car was in the parking lot. I hurried as fast as I could, not stopping to look around. I was running by the time I got to my car, and, after getting into my car,

I locked the doors, started the car and was on my way toward the street heading to my home.

First, I drove around several streets, making sure no one was following me. I drove up the alley behind my house. I drove into my garage, closed the garage door, then ran into the house.

Chapter 5

I headed for the bathroom, locked the door, then sat on the edge of the bathtub and tried to calm down.

I could hear the house phone ringing. I was sure my family wanted to know about my doctor's report. The call from my family helped calm me down.

I felt it was time to tell them about the man. They each sat in unbelievable silence while I described seeing the man, for the second time, and how he stared at me.

They, as my only family and caregivers, sat stunned, not knowing what to do or how to help me in this situation I was in. I had planned to stay at this house with them for a few months, trying to recuperate from my loss. Some of my family wondered if I was imagining all of this.

Some of my family felt I should stay in the house for a few more days, and they would not leave me alone. One or two of my family members would be with me. I readily agreed.

The whole world was passing me by while I stayed in the house and mourned. My family all wanted to get out of the house. It was suggested we all go out for lunch the following day. I knew I was drowning in my own self pity. So, I agreed to go out the next day.

I slept for the first time since my ordeal at the hospital seeing the man, and then in the parking lot.

The restaurant my family took me to was not high class but was one everyone felt relaxed in. The table my family asked for was just right for them. What I notice first was the very large TV. It was mostly for people loving to watch sports games with their friends. The TV was directly across from our table.

Our food was so delicious; we ere all eating and talking when the TV suddenly came on with a picture. My heart felt as if it had taken a great leap into my throat.

And I suddenly thought I was going to throw up my food I had just eaten.

The picture on the TV was of the man that had stared at me, then the TV was not saying a word.

The announcer began speaking, "This is a warning. If you see this man, do not do anything. Call the police immediately. He is a convicted criminal. He has killed two young women. He has escaped and is on the loose. Please lock your doors and windows. Let no one into your house that you do not know. If you are alone, find a friend to spend the night with. He is dangerous."

The whole restaurant was extremely quiet. Everyone was standing up and leaving food they had not eaten yet, heading out the door and going home.

I stood up fast. My family all stood up, and we walked toward the door. My family members surrounded me so I was protected.

Rushing out of the restaurant, the street was crowded and uncomfortable. Outside people were running toward their cars, They had been warned.

My family lost no time getting me into their car and driving me to the house. My family insisted I go to my room and lock the door after they had checked it. Then they went all through each room to make sure everything was clear. The basement was checked by each one.

The lights had been left off and only flashlights were used. A candle was lit on the kitchen table and then coffee was served.

I sat in the dark and listened to some of my family's conversation. They talked about this could be my imagination.

After everyone had gone to bed, I lay and listened to every creak and sound of an old house. I was cold and lonely.

I tried to avoid the news for the next few days. But, every time I walked by the TV or any conversation my family talked about was the man. The house remained dark even during the day time.

The man had been loose for four days. No one had seen him. The news reported he had left the area and was headed to his brother's in another state.

Every policemen on the town's force was looking for him.

Chapter 6

My family were all happy and all needed to get out of the house. Without too much argument, I was allowed to get out of the house. Walking out of the house and breathing in fresh air was nearly overwhelming.

The grocery store my family always shopped at was located in another city, miles from where we lived. I sat in the back in a seat by the window. I tried to enjoy getting out of the house. Feeling free, putting the man's face out of my mind. Just enjoying my family.

We drove by an old broken-down gas station, closed for many years. Standing by the station were three men. I was looking out of the car window while we drove by. One of the men looked right at me. I yelled, "It's him!"

My family all yelled back at me, "It's who?"

I screamed, "It's the man."

Not one family member believed me. I insisted we go immediately to the police station. The police quickly sent an unmarked car back to the old station and found no one there.

Needless to say, my family was concerned yet upset with me. I was disturbed. No one believed me.

After purchasing our groceries, we headed home. No one talked to me or looked at me but, they all looked at the old gas station as we drove by it.

I was again back in my bedroom that was dark and dreary, still believing I had seen the man and he had looked right at me.

The next few days nothing much was being said about the man. The police were still looking for him. I was still remembering his piercing eyes on me.

The house with all my family were all back to normal. Everyone doing their own responsibilities. I was not allowed outside unless someone was with me. The mail always came at the same time each day. My address was back home at my own house so I did not receive any mail until today.

A light knock on my door, then I heard a family member say, "You have a letter." In that second my body felt like it froze. I was so uncomfortable. I did not recognize the handwriting. It had only my name on the envelope, no return address. The envelope was small. The printing looked like a child's printing. I had no idea why I was feeling so nervous about this small letter. There were some smudges on the envelope, telling me something was very wrong.

I sat down on my bed fearing I would fall on the

floor. I slowly began opening the edges to pull out the letter, opening the small piece of paper inside the envelope.

I stared at it and read, "I see you." Nothing could have upset me more. I folded the paper back up and slipped it back into the envelope. I sat trying to control my mind and my shaking body.

I decided to show my family, then take it to the police station. My family took over and left for the police station.

I had no control of my mind. I crawled back into bed. I was so cold. I pulled the covers over me to try and get warm. I needed the covers over my head and closed my eyes. The man's face appeared instantly with his eyes staring at me.

Just then the door opened with my sister, Jill, walking up to my bed. She explained, she, Ruth and my brother, Ben, were taking me up to the cabin to keep me safe. My brother, Larry, would stay at the house. Jill also added we were leaving now.

Packing took only a short time, and we were on the road. I crawled in the back seat while the car was in the garage. I laid down in the back seat so no one could see that I was even in the car.

The trip was long and tiresome. My grandfather had left the cabin to my family. It was located in a desolated area. Trees surrounded the cabin with a small pond nearby. When my grandfather built the cabin, he bought all the land around so no one could settle near. There were no neighbors nearby for miles.

As children we came every summer to the cabin and spent nearly a month there. But, this was not a fun trip of laughter, swimming in the pond, and bonfires.

This trip was fear of losing my life. A trip of hiding from a man that had killed two young girls.

The cabin looked the same as we left it the last time we were here except for a few things. We all took notice of the things that were not in the same place. Ben immediately locked and bolted the door after we brought in all the groceries from the car.

There were two dirty dishes in the sink, a plate and a cup. Rugs had been moved. The bed covers were pulled up on the bed but not made like we left it.

No one said anything. We each looked at each other thinking the same thing. What if he, the man, had found our cabin?

I was so frightened all the time. My body jumped at every noise I heard. I could not stand to be alone. Jill or Ben had to be with me all of the time. We could sit outside if we were all together. No one ever spent time alone.

We had been there nearly a week when we all decided a swim in the pond would be what we all needed after being locked up in the cabin for a week. The day was warm, and the wind was calm.

We were all very good swimmers after growing up swimming each summer for a month. After the swim, we each sat laying back in our lounge recliners next to the pond.

I sat with my eyes closed, just resting and enjoying. I opened my eyes at the sound of a bird across the pond. I blinked my eyes a couple of times at what I thought I saw.

My body and mind were in an instant trauma. I made a terror sound. I yelled, "I saw the man, standing across the pond."

I pointed for Jill and Been to look. They did. Now they believed me. He had just stepped out in front of a large tree and looked right at me.

I jumped up. Jill and Ben also jumped up as I yelled, "It's him!" We ran to the cabin, locked and bolted the door.

Ben yelled, "Let's pack!" In only a short time, our suitcases sat by the door. The food was packed in the same boxes we brought it in. Everything was turned off.

Ben opened the door, ran to the car and lifted the trunk. Jill ran and started the car.

Chapter 7

It was only a short period of time, and we were on the road, back to our house. We stopped once for gas. Then, ate in the car as we drove.

While at the gas station, Ben called the police back home and told them, we saw the man. The police in this town were called, and they began the search for him.

It was all on the news again.

No one talked on the ride home. My sister and brother had also seen him, "the man." So, they truly believed me now.

It was nearly dark when we arrived home but Larry had all the lights on. I was ordered by Jill, Ruth and Larry to go immediately to my bedroom and told to lock the door.

I was so afraid of being alone and here I was, locked in my bedroom alone in the dark. I was sitting on my bed when I heard a noise at my window. I quickly got on my hands and knees and crawled to the window. I instantly saw a shadow standing outside of my window. I lowered my body down to the floor. Then I crawled to the door as fast as I could. I reached up to unlock my door.

I opened it just wide enough for me to crawl through. I continued to crawl toward my siblings. It was so quiet in the house. Something suddenly occurred to me. They were not in the house. They had left me along, thinking I was safe.

I heard a door squeak. It was the kitchen door. I crawled back to my bedroom, locked the door and crawled into my closet and under a pile of clothes I was going to give to the Goodwill.

Whoever it was came into the house, then tried to get into my bedroom. Suddenly, I could hear him running toward the kitchen door. My family had just driven into the driveway. The car lights could be seen shining into the house. Whoever it was saw the lights and ran to get out in a hurry. My family did not see anyone leave the house.

He, "The Man," is very clever and he knows the police are after him. Yet, he continues to hurt and destroy other people's lives. He is despicable, with no respect for another human being. He is ruthless, fearless, and he killed two young girls with so much hate in his heart.

Now, he has been in our house. I was being treated so cruelly. My body was uncontrollable.

I was screaming and yelling,"He's been here!"

My family came in the house in a hurry. All talking at once, saying how sorry they were for leaving me alone. They thought I was safe so they went to get something to eat.

The police were notified about "The Man" coming into our house. Again, we all told them what we knew. We were back were we had started.

"The Man" was fast and resilient. He had been sneaking in and out of people's homes for a very long time.

Chapter 8

My family decided to learn more about him and why he was so interested in me when I did not know him and had never seen him before that day in the medical building.

First, my family went to the police station. The information they heard and received was what "The Man" was charged with now. After learning his real name, Jill and Ben went to the city library that had newspaper articles about his horrible life on the run. They both had tablets and pens but they also ran off copies of all the write-ups about him, starting when he was a young boy. They brought all the information back to me.

His father and mother had not married. Neither his mother nor his father wanted to be held down by having to raise an unwanted baby. His grandmother consented to take care of him. His grandmother received a small amount of money for caring for him.

"The Man" ran away when he was thirteen years old and lived wherever he could. He ate from garbage thrown out from restaurants.

He was getting tougher each day, having to deal with old men on the streets. He struggled every day of his life. He was becoming extremely ruthless toward anyone he met on the street. He had no address so he did not attend school after thirteen years old.

Roberto Lee Diego had no education. He was made

fun of and treated unmercifully. To younger people he met on the street, "The Man" made it very clear he was always in charge. His famous words to them were "Don't mess with me."

Roberto's first thought each day was about survival. Finding food, water, and somewhere to sit and rest during the heat of the day, somewhere of his own so he would not get beat up taking someone else's spot. Then in the last time of the day, he had to worry about finding a safe place to sleep.

Roberto was always afraid at night. People would steal anything you had, and you never got it back.

Being clean was not a worry. If you were near water, a river or lake, you could wash off. If you could sneak into a gas station bathroom that was not locked, you could wash up in a hurry before getting caught. Everyone became aware of a sign in the window of most restaurants and stores stating you had to purchase something in order to use the bathroom. Most of the street people had no money to purchase anything.

His clothes were always too big for him. He found clothes people left along the street or he'd sneak into tents when guys were out looking for food. His clothes never fit right. He always had to roll up the shirt sleeves and pant cuffs. His hair grew long. At last he tied it back with a torn old rag.

Roberto started stealing small things. It made him happy he could do it so well. He would steal from anyone that wasn't looking. He didn't care about the things he stole from other people. He just liked getting by doing it.

Chapter 9

For many years while he grew up, this was the way he lived. This was his life. "The Man" knew no one cared for him or about him.

Food became more of a problem when more street people showed up in his area. It was at this time, he met the first girl he became attracted to.

Roberto was totally happy for the first time. He felt someone really cared about him and talked to him. He changed a lot the days he was with her. He cleaned himself up. He found some clothes that fit better. He really wanted her to like him.

Paula Marise was there in the area only because her father was missing, and she came looking for him. Paula's life was not like Roberto's. She had everything a girl or woman could ask for.

Roberto had never seen anyone so beautiful. He worked so hard to get her to like him. He was getting more angry as time went by. One night after she found her father, and Roberto knew she was going to leave, he killed her in a very cruel way. Then he dumped her body in a drainage ditch by the camp he was living in.

The murder had not been solved for a very long time, not until after Roberto Lee Diego had killed another young woman.

The camp Roberto was living in was growing larger every night so he decided to move.

Chapter 10

The next camp was deep inside the city. Roberto found a quiet place where he quickly took up residence. He had a tent he had taken from someone who had moved on and left it. Nothing changed for him until he met Rosa Shepard.

She lived in the camp and could take care of herself until she met Roberto Lee Diego. Roberto's tent was located next to hers. According to the picture of the second girl, she had left a nice home and had nowhere else to live but on the street. She had left because of a problem with her mother.

Rosa Shepard learned to be strong, learned to find food, learned how to find bathrooms to clean up in. She was bitter over her life, until she met Roberto. He talked to her about his hard life and could calm her down.

Roberto told her how many times he was beaten up by older men, how many nights he did not sleep, afraid someone would kill him. He admitted to Rosa how he cried a lot when he found a place to hide. He also told her how much he hated everyone he met or saw.

Everything he told her seemed to soften her heart. Roberto was falling in love with her. Rosa Shepard was so busy working the street, she had little time to return his affection. She would leave early in the morning with her sign and large paper cup. She walked in the middle of the highway between lights and panhandled. When she finally came back to camp, she was tired.

It was quoted in the newspaper Jill and Ben read how Roberto was really getting so frustrated about her coolness. One night Rosa came back to camp and told Roberto she had met someone that very day.

Nothing could have surprised him or hurt him more. He tried not to show his disappointment in her. After all the time he had spent trying to help her and then falling in love with her.

Roberto tried to be patient with Rosa. After Rosa got back to the camp later each night, he knew she had met someone and was sure she was with this new man.

Roberto's anger began to build in him. She did not love him or care about him. He knew that now.

They had always met for breakfast each morning and talked about what had happened to them the evening before. Roberto could tell Rosa had other things on her mind.

After Rosa left to go to her panhandling, Roberto began to make plans in his head. She was not going to run off with another man. He loved her.

Roberto lay in his tent that very night making a plan. He cleaned out his tent. He left no fingerprints. Her tent was next to his so he laid awake waiting for her. It was 2:30 a.m. when he heard her crawl into her tent.

Roberto crawled over to hers. He whispered her name several times. When she finally answered, he asked her if she would go for a short walk out of the camp. At first, she said, "No." Then she said, "Only a short one" as she was tired.

Roberto took her hand and they walked out of the camp and along the park. Then down along the river. He knew exactly where he was taking her. The rocks where he had left them.

Roberto stopped behind her, picked up one rock and struck her head as hard as he could. Rosa fell next to the water. He slipped all the rocks under her shirt and then kicked her body into the river. Her body went under the water quickly.

Roberto went back to his tent and tore it down. He tore Rosa's tent down, wrapped all her belongings up in it. He dug up the ground to get rid of any fingerprints, like he had done under his tent. He made it look like they had left together. He dropped all of her stuff in the burn barrel and made sure it caught fire.

Chapter 11

Roberto strapped his tent onto his back and started to walk away from the area. He found a place to hide until dark. Then he would walk as far away as he could. Roberto did this each day and night.

Everyone in the camp thought what he wanted them to think. That they had left together. No one reported them.

I read every article Jill and Ben handed me. I spent the whole day in shock and feeling fear for my life.

I was afraid before but now I was petrified. Not knowing where to go from here. Was there a safe place for me? The police could not find him or catch him. Why was he seeking me out? I had done nothing to hurt him.

Chapter 12

Ruth announced she was sleeping with me. I could not have been happier. I put all the information I had about Roberto in my dresser drawer so it was out of my sight.

The phone ringing early in the morning woke Ruth and me up. Larry answered it was in the kitchen so we could not hear his conversation. It was the police calling to tell us Roberto had been seen by a visitor in the park. The police, of course, did not get there in time. It was him. He was gone. Sometimes people see someone looking similar and think he is someone else, they said.

The park was only a short distance from our home. I was extremely upset but my family was upset also. We huddled together to talk about what we were going to do next.

Roberto had been on the street for such a long time. He had friends that would help him. Street people are always under a lot of threats. Fights break out frequently but if one of them needed help, most every street person would help immediately.

According to one article written, that is where Roberto was hiding. The article stated Roberto had one good friend. He would always go to when he was in trouble. No one had any idea who the street person was or where he was located.

Nothing changed in the next two weeks. I felt beings there was no news about Roberto on the TV or radio, I could go back to work. I approached my family on the subject. No one could agree. I told them I would wait another week. I called my boss. He informed me my sick leave was almost up, and I would have to return to work in a week.

That afternoon the doorbell rang. Larry went to the door and a policeman was standing there. He came to inform us Roberto Lee Diego had been arrested in another state. Nothing could have been better to hear for all of my family but especially me.

We all began to make plans on what we would do the rest of the day, and the rest of the week before everyone went back to their own homes.

My life had changed again. I went back to feeling almost normal. One by one my family was leaving to go back to their own home. To a way of life they had before they came to stay with me.

Chapter 13

I returned to work, and it felt so good to drive again and not be afraid. But, I couldn't help looking at everyone along the street.

I loved my job as a head nurse. It kept me very, very busy, constantly at the desk.

One day the phone rang, and my mind was so busy with work, I grabbed the phone and said the name of the hospital. The voice on the other end nearly made me drop the phone and run for help.

"The Man" said, "Margaret, is that you? I've been watching you." Then he hung up.

I called the police and told them who I thought it was. They first said, "It was not him. They had him in jail. He'd been caught." Then the police called later and said, "It was not him they had him in jail."

So, Roberto Lee Diego was still running free.

After telling my superior the news, I left and drove home, shaking all the way. Roberto knew all about me.

The police called my house phone and told me Roberto made the call from a payphone in my neighborhood. But after the police investigated, he had disappeared. The entire police force was out looking for him but they could not find him..

Ruth came to stay with me while my others siblings went back to work. I was in a terrible predicament. I had to quit my job. He was ruining my life. I would have to live on my inheritance.

The police were looking through every camp, including under the city where there were so many hiding places. There were so many bridges in this area with homeless camps.

I stayed in my bedroom the first few days after I quit my job. Then Ruth insisted I come out to the kitchen for coffee with her. A small feeling of relief rushed over me. I talked to Ruth for the first time about my life being torn apart.

Not only what I'd been going through but how this all started with Roberto Lee Diego.

Ruth brought the mail in each day at the same time. Today was no different. Ruth walked out to my mailbox and then hurried back into the house as if she saw something she was upset about.

Ruth ran into the kitchen and handed me the mail. Laying on top of the letters was a picture of my house.

I turned the picture over and written on the back was, "I noo whair u liv."

Ruth and I sat down at the kitchen table and looked at each other. No words came out of my mind. The first thing I did was to call the police. They took all of my information and said they would get back to me.

The rest of the day was heartbreaking and confusing to me. Not knowing what to do next. Ruth tried to help me the best she could, to calm me down.

The police called later in the day and mentioned how they had nothing to report.

The police dropped by my house and picked up the picture. They took it back to the police station to test it for fingerprints.

Everything was again at a standstill.

Ruth was becoming impatient. She expressed to me she was ready to go look for Roberto Lee Diego herself. I was sure she was the one that could find him.

A few days always passed before Roberto made contact with me. The days were slipping by, and the police thought it was time for Roberto to contact me. They asked me if they could leave a police car on the street near my house. I agreed, of course.

With the darkness of night time also came a severe thunderstorm with thunder and lightning. I could not sleep that night. Suddenly, I was aware of someone outside my window. Thinking it was the police, I went to the window. Standing very close was a man looking in at me.

The police also saw the man at my window. The man was caught and arrested. He was taken downtown. We were so excited thinking it was Roberto Lee Diego, and this was all over.

The police called, telling me the man was a street person. No connection to Roberto. But, he had admitted a man he did not know asked if he would go to my house after dark and look in a particular window in my house.

The police also stated the man was drunk. He had drugs on him and no money. He also appeared to have dementia. They just had to let him go. He could not tell the police anything else.

So, now the police would have to wait for Roberto Lee Diego to contact me again.

It was the same amount of days when Roberto made his move.

Suddenly, the most high-pitched whistles were blowing and could be heard all over town. Ruth and I searched each window to look for smoke. Then it sounded as if the fire trucks, police cars and the ambulances were all going out of town.

Ruth never left my side. She was standing close enough to me I could hear her breathing. She turned her head and looked directly into my eyes and said, "I smell smoke."

The fright I felt instantly triggered my body. I began to shiver so badly. I had to sit down in the nearest chair.

Ruth began to yell, "Fire! Fire in the back porch!" We were both panicking.

I yelled, "Call the fire department!"

Ruth had been calling over and over, and the answer was always the same, "The fire department is all out on call, and the ambulances are out on call."

Chapter 14

The smoke was coming in under two of the doors leading from the porch into the house. In our state of shock, for seconds, Ruth and I stood and watched the smoke come in. Then Ruth yelled, "I see fire on the kitchen wall!"

I screamed, "What if Roberto is out there?"

"Margaret, all of our neighbors are out there, too," said Ruth. "He won't hurt you even if he is out there because of all the people trying to help us put the fire out that is burning your house down. Now come on, Margaret!"

All the neighbors had their hoses on the fire, and it was nearly out. The porch was nearly burned off and the kitchen's outer wall was scorched.

The neighbors were all asking, "How did the fire start?"

My first thought was to tell them all about Roberto

but I didn't think they would understand about him.

So I told them all, "The fire department will investigate."

The fire marshal came to see me at Jill, Ruth and Ben's house where I was staying until my house was rebuilt.

He explained, "The neighbors had seen two old street men in your backyard before the fire started."

I stood listening to something I was not surprised to hear. Roberto was going to get me, one way or another, and no one knew how to stop him.

Chapter 15

Once again my family was back to trying to protect me. We were now all at Larry's house. They never left me alone. They took turns staying with me. Jill and Ruth took turns sleeping with me. If I left the bedroom, Larry and Ben stood beside me at all times.

Time was slipping away as usual and the time for Roberto to do something again was now here.

The house was always locked up tight. The doors, all of the windows, on the main floor and on the second floor.

We felt they were secure.

The only thing that could not be locked was Larry's garage. We had been in the house for over three days when Larry stated we needed to go through the drive-in. The decision was unanimous.

With only one thought on my mind: keeping us all safe.

I said to Larry, "I really don't think you should use the car. The garage was the only place we could not lock."

Larry responded by saying, "Ben and I will go check the car."

Ben and Larry went into the garage. They hurried through the kitchen and then opened the door into the garage. When they both came back into the house, they were nervous and showing stress. Both started talking at the same time.

Finally it occurred to each one, no one was understanding what the other one was saying. Larry started first, "Roberto or his buddies were in my garage. There's no doubt."

"What we found was the brake pads were destroyed on all of the wheels. I wouldn't be able to stop no matter how I tried," Larry continued. "We could have been killed or I could have killed someone."

My siblings all stood looking shocked and were upset, more upset then when they witnessed the fire. Each one of my siblings was breathing so hard. The air was thick and heavy in the kitchen.

Jill, Ruth and I put our arms around each other for support. Ben and Larry were talking to each other loudly.

I heard Ben say, "We have to call in more help. We need to talk to the FBI for help."

Everyone stopped talking after what Ben said. All agreed.

Ben was excited and continued thinking and talking. "We will have to call a taxi until my car is repaired. We need to hire a detective to help before Roberto kills one of us."

It was suddenly dead quiet in the room. They were all listening to Ben.

Ben and Larry called for a taxi and went to the police station, hoping to hear some good news. Every police officer the town had was out looking for Roberto. Every FBI agent was out looking for Roberto.

Roberto was very smart, clever and resourceful. He had the very brilliant street person helping him hide. He also had the same kind of people helping him destroy my life. I was on the edge of a breakdown, thinking what a horrible situation Roberto will put me in or do to me.

Ben and Larry hired a detective ,and we all sat down and told Clarence Miller all we knew about Roberto Lee Diego. We hired Clarence for one week.

Clarence was a large built man. He wore his hair in a long ponytail. He was sincere and sympathetic to me. He wrote down everything the five of us told him. I couldn't help but like him for his interest in stopping Roberto. For all the damage and pain Roberto had caused me.

His last statement to me was, "I will contact you as soon as I find out something. No matter what it is."

Chapter 16

We had four days, the usual amount of days between the hurtful things Roberto did to me. The fear in my heart was growing more each hour. I stayed in the house with Ruth by my side.

I spent time thinking of my siblings. I would rather he hurt me than to hurt one of them.

It was late the second night after we hired Clarence Miller. He knocked softly on the door. Ben went to the door but before he opened the door, he instructed all of us to go into my bedroom and lock the door.

It was Clarence at the door. He had to tell Ben who he was before Ben would let him in. He was so dirty! He was dressed in an old shirt that was torn as well as pants with larges holes starting above his knees to his mismatched shoes. His socks were two different colors as well.

Ben ushered him into my bedroom that was dark. We stood and listened to him whisper about how he thought he was getting close to finding Roberto's hiding place. Roberto was hiding under the city where the old railroad ran.

But, he also discussed his concern for each one of

us, telling us to sneak out the back of the house, walk a few blocks and call a taxi. He wanted us to stay in a motel for the night.

After Clarence left, we did exactly what he said.

This was the first night I had slept for a very long time. I felt safe with my siblings. I was not in Larry's house where Roberto could get at me.

We all took the same route back to Larry's house. Upon entering the back porch, we all stepped in and stood looking at each other. We all heard the same noise.

We all looked at each other. Then we began to look around the porch. Nothing was out of place. We went slowly into the living room, looking all over, including under the furniture and in every corner.

Jill and I went into my bedroom. We both saw it at the same time. I wanted to scream but Jill screamed as loud as she could. We slammed the door behind us. Just then, my siblings all came together, and Larry yelled, "Get out of the house!" It took us only seconds and we were all out the door and in the backyard.

Larry and Ben were calling an exterminator. The house was filled with snakes! Larry explained to the exterminator to come through the garage. Then into the kitchen through the door that had been broken into.

Roberto had won again.

My siblings refused, including me, to stay and sleep in the house that night. We all returned to the motel.

Even knowing the exterminator finished cleaning the house of all the snakes, we were nervous staying there. But, we did it for Larry and returned to his house the next day.

We sat around the table and discussed again what we would do in four days. Nothing seemed to work. We had no idea what we would do next.

The four days passed and we heard nothing. Nothing unusual happened, nor did we hear from Clarence.

The fourth day started the same as the last three. My siblings were all watching over me. It was late in the morning when we heard a knock at the door. Larry jumped up from his chair. He opened the door only a small way and found his neighbor standing there.

"Larry," she said. "The mailman put this letter in my mailbox by mistake. Your name is on the envelope." She handed the letter to Larry, then turned and started home.

Larry looked down at the writing on the envelope. Suddenly, he was reminded of the printing on the letter I had gotten from Roberto.

Larry did not hesitate. He brought the letter right to me. I slowly reached out and took the letter. After I saw the printing, I knew who it was from.

By this time, my siblings were all yelling at me to open the letter.

My heart was pounding. My hands were shaking,

and I handed the letter to Ben.

I noticed Ben's hands were also shaking but he managed to get the letter opened. Then he handed the letter back to me.

It was devastating for me but I knew it was addressed to me. And, putting it on my siblings was not right. They had done so much for me.

The letter read: "U pye mee 10000.00 drap of 27 St NOOWW."

I read it many times. I could recite it by heart.

I did not have $10,000 without my inheritance. But I would have to so my family would not get hurt. I breathed in a large amount of air for some relief, then let it out slowly. I had to do this.

27 Street was a well-known hangout for street people. Each of my siblings took the letter, studied it, memorized what Roberto had written.

Larry was adamant we call Clarence Miller on his cell phone and tell him about the letter. Clarence replied he would come to the house. He also said he would come in through the back door.

Chapter 17

When Clarence arrived, we all met in my bedroom so we would not be seen by anyone walking by the house.

Clarence mentioned this would never be over if I paid Roberto the money he asked for. But, on the other hand, he could and would hurt one of us.

Clarence added Roberto would always keep asking for more money. Clarence went on to say, he would deliver the money if I decided to pay Roberto. He told us he would hide and watch who picked up the money. He'd follow Roberto or have an FBI agent follow him and hope the street man would lead us to Roberto.

Then I asked Clarence, "What do you do? You can't arrest the street man because Roberto will not get the money." Then I added, "I cannot afford to pay him again."

"We have to find Roberto and arrest him," Clarence said with anger in his voice. "Because, if you pay Roberto and he gets away, he will continue to pressure you for more money wherever he is hiding. He will continue to threaten you and your family."

Suddenly, it was very quiet in my bedroom. We did not have the answer nor did we know what to do.

The following morning I drove to the bank with Jill and Ruth. I asked to draw out the amount of money Roberto was asking for. Getting the money for Roberto was the only choice I had. If one of my siblings got hurt or worse, I could never live with myself. I had to do this.

I told Clarence exactly when I would return with the money so he could pick it up.

Clarence came into Larry's house looking unrecognizable to pick up the $10,000. I wrapped it tightly in a brown paper bag.

He left the house looking disgusted, hurt he hadn't caught Roberto yet. He was agitated, and more determined than he'd ever been.

Before Clarence drove down to the meeting place with Roberto, he notified the police and the FBI where to go and the time to be there.

Clarence drove within two blocks of 27th Street, left his car and walked the rest of the way. A culvert was the entrance to the underground hiding area for street people. He found a small space next to the opening.

Clarence sat down, pulled an old blanket that was laying there over him and tried to hide. Two hours passed, and there was no movement anywhere. Then Clarence heard a noise sounding like footsteps coming toward him. He stood up and held the paper bag so it could be seen.

A man came right up to Clarence and said, "Is that for me?"

"Is your name Roberto?" Clarence asked in a rather loud angry voice.

The man answered saying, "I'm to take the package to someone that asked me for a favor."

Just then, two FBI men approached, dressed like street men. They told the man who they were and that he should let them deliver the bag. Scaring the man by telling him he could go to jail, the man told them reluctantly where to take the bag.

The man turned the package over, handing it to one of the FBI agents. He turned and ran further into the tunnel as fast as he could. Clarence could not see him within seconds.

What the men did not know was he was heading toward Roberto to warn him. In this situation, friends take good care of each other. They were not told about Roberto being a killer, only that he needed help.

Clarence was searching all the way to the opening of the culvert. He was mad and upset. He just wanted to get out for some fresh air. He had the bag of money. He knew now the man warned Roberto. The two FBI agents left in anger as well. They would have to start all over and wait to hear from Roberto.

Clarence called Larry and asked if he could come to explain what had happened, that he had the money, and how we would have to wait to hear from Roberto again.

Everything was on hold again. Everyone was on hold as well: the police, FBI, Clarence, my siblings and me.

Chapter 18

I knew we had four days and then we'd hear from

Roberto. It always took him that length of time to set up his hold on me. The fourth day the phone rang. Larry answered it, hung up the phone and went directly into the garage while we all stood and watched.

Larry came hurrying back into the kitchen where we all were crouched down waiting. He handed me two tickets. I carefully read the tickets. They were for a train ride into a big city north of us. I knew exactly what Roberto wanted me to do: bring the bag of money on the train.

Clarence called. He was on the way to Larry's house. He came in clean shaven and all dressed up. After hearing and seeing the tickets, he told me he was going. He needed a woman to go with him but it would not be me. With no hesitation, Ruth insisted she go. Clarence made a phone call and asked for two policewomen to dress in street clothes and ride the train with him but pretend they did not know him.

This time they were going to do it differently. They would take the street person to the police station and interrogate him in case he knew where Roberto was hiding.

The train was scheduled to leave in two hours. Everyone was planning to leave on the train when Clarence was ready. Clarence had the money in a small suitcase.

The policewomen were asked to sit four seats behind and diagonal from Clarence and Ruth. They were to watch everyone in the train car.

Clarence and Ruth sat looking like a couple traveling on a holiday trip. No one in the train car would ever suspect they were being watched very carefully.

The train was beginning to pick up speed. Clarence decided to check out the other train cars. He saw one man that he felt did not belong on this expensive train.

Clarence set back down next to Ruth, knowing someone had to give him more instructions. He needed to know where to drop off the money or who to give it to. This time he hoped it would be different.

The conductor walked by and handed Clarence a piece of paper. Clarence asked where it came from. All the conductor could tell him was a man in another train car gave it to him to give it to the man sitting in Seat No. Four, Car No. Two. The conductor couldn't remember which one now as he had walked through all the train cars.

Clarence quickly opened up the slip of paper, which said, "Leave the suitcase in the seat you're in and get off the train and go back where you came from."

Clarence had no other choice. He was hoping the two policewomen would be right there. And they were. They saw the same man Clarence had seen, looking disheveled. He had come up the aisle past them, gone right to the suitcase and picked it up. The two policewomen were there when he took one step away from the seat with the money in his hand. They arrested him and cuffed his hands behind his back.

Clarence and Ruth were with the two policewomen when they took the man to jail. He was the same man that Clarence had seen at the culvert.

The man was interrogated by the police and FBI. He told them he got paid to pick up the suitcase. He was to take it into the train station and put it in a locked box. So, that's what the police had him do. But, he was being closely watched by the police, FBI, and Clarence. Then he was taken back to jail so he couldn't talk to anyone.

Another street man picked up the suitcase from the locked box. But, the police were right there and arrested him. He said, "I got paid a small amount. I was to deliver to an old abandoned house." He gave the police the address.

Clarence dressed up like he lived on the street. He was dropped off a couple blocks from the old house. He walked, carrying the suitcase, pretending to limp.

Chapter 19

The police and FBI agents surrounded the block and some were as close as the backyard of the house next door.

Clarence pushed his body against the door and stepped into a foul-smelling room. Two men dressed in torn clothes, each holding a gun directed at Clarence.

Clarence blurted out, "I'm just here to deliver this suitcase! Here, take it!" He took a couple of steps toward the two men. A gun shot went off.

In less than one second, the room was filled with police and FBI agents. Clarence lay lifeless on the floor. There was total confusion in the room. The two men were on the floor face down while FBI agents were putting handcuffs on them.

An ambulance crew was attending to Clarence. Once the oxygen was applied, and the blood coming from the bullet entrance was stopped, he was loaded into the ambulance and transported to the nearest hospital.

The two street men were taken to the police station.

The police were irritated and tired. Not being able to catch Roberto, the interview of the two men was very hostile. The police were firm during questioning.

The two street men were so afraid of having to go to jail, they told all they knew. The man who did the shooting would be held for attempted murder. Clarence was still alive in the hospital.

The two men were separated so the police could get each man's story. The stories were nearly alike. They each got paid a small amount. But, the man with the gun would get more money for shooting Clarence because Roberto knew who he was.

Both men told the police Roberto was waiting under a large bridge on the edge of town.

Every policeman, every FBI agent and anyone dealing with police work was alerted to go to the bridge. No sirens were to be used. No driving up to the bridge. Everyone was to walk quietly for two or more blocks and surround the street people's camp.

The orders were to surround the bridge. Close in and not let one person out.

Larry, Ben, Jill and I arrived at the hospital as soon as I got word from the police department. Clarence was in an induced coma.

I begin to cry the minute I walked into his room. Jill was so emotional when she saw him, I couldn't help but think she was very interested and very concerned.

Each one of us bowed our head, then left the room to talk to the doctor. It was a relief to hear the doctor say Clarence's chances were very good. They would wake him in a couple of days.

Chapter 20

All the street people under the large bridge were unaware they were surrounded. The police and FBI agents were standing shoulder to shoulder. If Roberto was in the camp, he was going to be caught this time.

Each street person was checked carefully.

A terrible fight broke out when a man tried to break though the tight circle of men holding in all the street people. The more they fought, the more people joined in, wanting to fight the police and FBI. The fighting was a complete disaster for the police and FBI agents. One man broke out and started running down the highway.

He would have gotten away if the two policewomen hadn't studied his picture. They knew immediately who it was, and they went after him. It took both of them to bring him down and put cuffs on him.

The jail cell was the only way the police could hold him. But, they needed to make an identification. I received a phone call asking me to come to the police station. They had who they thought was Roberto.

My heart was racing! My body said, "No." but my head said, "You have to do this." Roberto was a murderer. He must never be able to hurt anyone else the rest of his life.

My siblings all walked into the police station with me. I asked if the police would put Roberto in a lineup so he could never look at me again.

I took one look at the lineup, and I told the police the number Roberto was standing in. It was all over.

I had my life back. I could go to my own home, get my job back and just live my life again. The money was all given back to me.

Chapter 21

I opened all the windows in my house and let a cool, clean breeze blow through my house. It was the first time for a very long time.

I sat down in my favorite chair, laid my head back and my mind began to drift back to when this all started.

The whole episode wasn't about me personally. It was something about my face, hair or the way I was dressed that day. Something triggered a memory of hate or rejection from someone in his past and he immediately disliked me.

My siblings and I had read his life story, written by a reporter who had no idea how I felt or what I went through. He only knew about Roberto Lee Diego's history. The two young women he killed did not have a personal story about each one. All of his life he had been pushed away.

But hurting people is not what is right, and that is what he did to anyone that crossed him. Or, like me, reminded him of someone in his past.

A large writeup and a picture of Roberto came out in the town's newspaper a few days after the all-out conjoined effort by the police, FBI and everyone connected to law enforcement.

I looked at the picture and my whole body was affected. It was going to take me a long time to get over what had happened to me.

His dark eyes looked out at me as if he were seeing only me. I quickly folded the paper up and went to my closet. I found an empty drawer in a dresser, and on the very bottom, I threw the paper in, and, closed the drawer forever.

The End

WHERE'S MY BABY?

by Phyllis A. Collmann

Chapter 1

By the time I was six years old, I knew I wanted to be a policeman, or as I am a woman, I wanted to be a policewoman.

My mother named me Josephine, but, my father called me Jo. That was the closest he could get to having a boy.

My father was a police officer. He started sharing stories with me when I was first able to walk. I sat every afternoon when he came home and listened, enraptured by his daily adventures. My father had a way of making each story fascinating and exciting to a little girl.

His love for protecting and helping people was very inspiring. I learned it early in my life. I couldn't wait to grow up to work as a policewoman.

My life was as normal as any other little girl's growing up. We went to many programs the police department put on and was involved in.

I joined all of the girls' clubs and then my father thought I should learn karate. I loved it! I earned my black belt after three years of study. I also joined the Girl Scouts.

I studied incredibly hard the last year of high school and learned all I could.

My graduation was perfect. Family, friends, and neighbors all turned out for my party. I was so happy and relieved after graduation.

But that evening, things changed.

Chapter 2

My father was waiting for the party to be over to tell me his news. He insisted I do two years in the Army for all the training before entering the police academy. My shock must have shown on my face.

He was convinced this was the right course of action. His thinking was that I needed to have the physical training the Army provided. He wanted me to get in the best shape of my life before studying to be a police officer.

I thought I could handle the two years. I could not say no. He was almost a perfect father, and I trusted him with my life. But, in reality, I wasn't prepared for how difficult the training would be.

The marching, climbing, swimming and running dressed in full gear were at times unrelenting and then there was the classwork.

At no time did I have an opportunity to go out and celebrate with any of my friends. Eventually they all stopped asking me to go with them for a weekend of drinking and dancing. They came back to the barracks, staggering, laughing, and talking nonsense.

I always pretended to be asleep, and they left me alone. The only good that came out of my not having any fun was my marks were superior compared to the rest of my unit.

By this time, I was ready and determined to graduate at the top of the class. And I did just that. I was even asked to speak.

My commanding officer asked me to tell everyone how well the female soldiers were treated. A kind, loving speech.

I only had a short period of time to get it written. So, sleep was not a top priority for a couple of days. I also had to pack and clean up my space, including under my bed. My whole unit had to pass inspection by the unit leader. Fortunately, we passed and were all free to go.

I was now ready to write my speech for graduation. There were so many thoughts swimming around in my head.

What I really wanted to say and what I was allowed to say were two different things.

I had to admit I was so much stronger than I had ever been. This ended up good for me because of the police work I planned to enter into. I was going to be the best policewoman I could be.

Chapter 3

My family poured into the auditorium that was

chosen to hold graduation for five units of soldiers. There were bands, flag carriers, airplanes flying over, and speeches by all of the top brass. It was exciting and helped me realize it was part of my route to a dream I had all of my life.

The whole service had only a few problems. Everyone seemed happy with how it all worked out. It was long but worthwhile to sit on a very hard seat.

Families greeted their own with hugs and kisses, more hugs and more kisses.

My family all showed me how proud they were of me. My father had tears in his eyes. I had never seen that before. My mother always cried at everything I did. She cried happy tears when I drew very bad pictures in the first grade. I thought that was normal. Every mother should cry over pictures their child drew.

I stood in front of my father in my uniform. I wondered for a quick second if he wished he was looking at a son instead of a skinny, five-foot-seven daughter. But, he really looked happy. So, I put the thought out of my mind and enjoyed the moment.

The gift from my parents was a nice used car. Another lesson I was taught was don't spend it if you don't have it. They had money but they were very conservative with it.

I dearly loved having my own car.

Chapter 4

I rested for two weeks, then applied to enter the police academy. It took a few days to receive an answer. But, I was sure when they checked my last name, it would be a sure admittance. My father was one of the top officers in the department.

I did not know what to expect but after the Army training, I knew this was what I wanted. I had wanted this all of my life!

I looked around my class, and I knew I could whip all but one. He was tall and had muscles, telling me he worked out before getting into the program. And he was very nice looking.

I learned in class his name was Shurman. The day we had open class, we were encouraged to tell something about ourselves. I said my last name. I knew I might be treated dreadfully and kidded a lot and I was.

Shurman never said a word to me nor even looked at me. But, I was attracted to him. There was just something about him.

After class, I walked out slowly and hoped he would say something to me. He said, "Hey!" and walked right passed me. I had to be thankful and decided this was going to take me a long time. We were half way through the first year before any contact happened between us.

We were all in the gym learning how to defend

ourselves from a rough, tough, horrible killer. I really thought he would be gentle when I was matched up with him. When I found how rough after he grabbed me, I knew I had to defend myself and try to beat him. I fought him with all of my Army training strength. Believe me, he did not expect it. I had him down on the mat and was on top before he even realized I had beaten him.

The look on his face was definitely not happy. I crawled off of him, and the coach held my arm in the air, making him look bad.

I could not tell if it was hate or a lesson well learned. Never trust an Army brat, a Girl Scout, or a karate champion with a black belt.

Showing all the class he was not a poor loser, he came over and shook my hand.

I spoke first and said, "I'm sorry."

He answered saying, "Why are you sorry? You won."

"I know," I said, "but I really did not want to."

Shurman walked away in front of the class, smiling, letting them think he let me win.

I bowed my head and whispered, "Thank you, Dad." I really thought I would never say that.

Class was out, and I had a lot of studying to do. We were all going to the shooting range in the morning.

If he had stopped and told me he had let me win, I was going to jump on him again. But, instead he said, "Would you do me the honor of having a cup of coffee with me?"

I opened my mouth and had a hard time speaking. Instead of saying, "I would love to!" I said, "Yes. Thank you."

He told me where to drive, and I did. I parked and he was waiting for me. After a few minutes it got easier to talk, and we, or I, had fun. He acted totally different than when he was in class.

He admitted he hated looking weak in front of the class. I tried to convince him everybody in class was intimidated by him. He couldn't believe it. He was okay with it but he had a hard time believing it. After that, he was more relaxed and easier to talk to.

He offered to pay for my coffee and roll but I insisted I pay for my own. I did not know if he had money for his police classes or not. I only knew my father was paying for mine.

When we said goodnight, I asked, "I did win, didn't I?" His answer was just a big grin. Then he walked away to his old worn-out pickup.

I drove home doubting myself now. I really liked him anyway. But, somehow I had to beat him at something.

In the morning we were all to meet at the shooting range. My father had taught me how to shoot by the time I was ten years old. I really loved competing against my father. He always won until I was fifteen. I could beat him every time we were at the range. I must admit I loved it!

I even though of letting Shurman win but then I thought about my father and knew in my heart he would be disappointed with me.

I arrived early that morning and found my name card and shooting position. I quickly looked at the name on each side of me, relieved Shurman would not be standing next to me.

The voice over the intercom was loud and clear. The officer instructed us all to put our safety glasses on, ear plugs in, and load our gun. Then he instructed us to raise our guns to shoot. He yelled, "Ready. Aim. Fire." Everything went as well as instructed.

We were to shoot five bullets. We were to shoot, reload and shoot again as fast as we could.

We were then to lay down our gun and walk to the waiting room. The large cardboard targets were automatically pulled up and checked.

I felt comfortable. I could see where my bullets had gone into the cardboard. I couldn't help but feel discomfort in my stomach, wondering how Shurman had done.

The officer's voice came over the loudspeaker saying we could go back to the police station and wait for the results. I left alone to drive back to the station. I couldn't help but notice the look on each person's face getting out of their cars. It was so important to our career to score high.

As I was driving, I began to wonder if I was liking Shurman more than I really should. I really did not know him that well.

I sat waiting in my assigned seat. Shurman walked in. He smiled at me and said, "Hey." I smiled more than I should have. I secretly hoped he had beaten me in the shooting test.

The officers all came into class and began to tell how well everyone had done. They went on to say, police work is knowing how to shoot a gun; not always to kill or hurt someone, but, to keep control.

I was listening to every word, then suddenly I heard an officer call my name. At that point, I didn't want to hear it. He asked me to come up to the front of the class. My heart not only was beating very rapidly but I felt pain.

I could feel every eye in the room on me as I stood up. The room was so quiet, it was like everyone had even stopped breathing. I realized I could even get my own breath.

The officer put his hand out and with a booming voice said, "Congratulations and great job!" Then he added, "You were first. Class dismissed."

I stumbled back to my chair like I was half drunk. As I passed Shurman, he said, "Let's have coffee."

Chapter 5

I got into my car and drove to the coffee shop. I

found our usual table, sat down, and ordered two cups of coffee. Shurman sat down smiling. He looked relaxed and not upset like I thought he would be.

Looking across the table at him, I knew I had fallen in love with him. I had no way of knowing how he felt about me. Up to now, he acted like he could be my brother. I noticed he was staring at me like he didn't know how he felt about me. It seemed as if I was a challenge to him. I think he liked a woman less aggressive, more gentle and mild.

But, the influence my father had on me while growing up made me stand on my own two feet, and I was very strong.

I was aware Shurman was not raised in this area. My concern was he'd leave and go back to his home and the community he came from.

Our conversation started on our classes winding down and then what our choice of police work we each would prefer. We had both decided we would like to be detectives.

I did not let him know how very happy I was that he had decided on the same career I would like to pursue. But, I wondered where he was going to pursue his career. I knew I'd stay in the community I was raised in.

We sat quietly for awhile, drinking our coffee. Then Shurman said, "I've decided to stay on here. I think there is a lot of work here."

I tried hard to show no emotion but I was extremely happy. The smile on my face gave me away. This was the first time he showed me any sign he truly like me. He reached over, took my hand and covered my hand with his.

Shurman walked with his arm around my waist while he walked me to my car. I could not have been happier.

I invited Shurman to come to my home to meet my parents and have dinner with us. The look on his face told me no. He wasn't ready and couldn't do it yet. It took two weeks and then he agreed to it.

It turned out to be a good evening. We spent more time together, and I knew I was deeply in love with him. He was kind and gentle when he touched me.

Chapter 6

The classes were finished for both of us, and we were out on the street. We worked the late shift, checking doors, moving street people in order to clear the street, and making young people go home for the night.

It was what we thought our careers would be like but we were both determined to do what it took to keep going.

It was a night of summer heat. The buildings with no air conditioning kept everyone outside until after midnight.

We had a radio call about a young woman having a baby out on the street. When we arrived, we found her laying on the cement having contractions.

She was a teenager. She looked scared and in much pain. I called for an ambulance with her hollering not to do it. I rode in the ambulance with her. She swore at me, striking out at me while we made our way to the hospital.

Shurman was to meet me there.

The baby arrived only a few minutes after getting her in a bed. She continued to swear at me while I told her she had a beautiful baby boy.

I gave the nurse my name and told her to call me if something went wrong with either the mother or the baby. The mother refused to give the nurses her name or any information about herself.

Shurman and I went back to the police station and wrote out our entire report. We were both disappointed with the young mother and could not believe how badly she had acted.

What a horrible way for a baby to start his life!

The next morning the sound of my phone ringing woke me after a really restless night of sleep. The voice on the other end was panicked, yelling the mother had left the hospital, leaving the baby behind.

I explained I would report to the police station, then come to the hospital. I quickly called Shurman and he said he would meet me at the hospital. All I could think of was of the mother with nothing had left with nothing, leaving a beautiful baby boy behind.

I stood looking at the baby, and suddenly I wanted the baby as my own. I realized all of the paperwork involved in wanting him, but I wanted him anyway.

Shurman stood looking at me. Then he said, "Don't you have to be married to do something like this?"

I answered saying, "What do you suggest I do?"

He had a funny smile on his face and without skipping a beat, he said, "Would you marry me?"

I was really caught off guard. But, as quickly as he'd asked, I answered, "Yes!"

On our way back to the police station, we stopped at the Public Defender's Office and told the judge we wanted to get married. It took another thirty minutes before we stood in front of the judge as well as his wife as the witness.

We spoke our wedding vows, and we were married within the hour. Everything moved right along. The police chief called the hospital and instructed them to care for the baby until the paperwork was done.

The lawyer we hired was quick to do all the documentation. He delivered the adoption papers to the head of the hospital. Everything was in but we didn't know if he was ours. We had to wait two weeks to see if someone came to claim him. After that time, we could take the baby home. We had good credentials and we were approved.

Chapter 7

Shurman refused to move into my parents' home. So we quickly hunted for a home. The one we found was perfect for us. My bedroom furniture was moved into the empty house. We both loved it! We stayed in bed until noon the next day.

Making love was new to both of us. I had been in love with him for a very long time. His gentle touch made my body want him even more. I responded to everything he wanted. His kisses covered my body. His tongue made lovemaking out of this world.

We drove to the cafe for coffee. Shurman wanted to talk about the baby boy. He said he loved the baby, too. We shopped for baby clothes, diapers and a crib.

I had seen guys get excited in the academy about their girlfriends and when they had a baby. Shurman was a man in love with a new baby coming into his life, and he was ecstatic.

We hadn't decided on a name for the baby yet. A name was still being talked over, and a decision was yet to be made.

My parents shopped for anything we forgot. The nursery was painted light blue, and the curtains were bright blue. It looked perfect for bringing a baby boy home to. Shurman tested the baby monitor so we could hear our baby boy cry.

I wanted the days to move faster until the two weeks were up. A week had passed when my phone started ringing early in the morning.

I answered the phone to a man's voice stating my husband and I should come to the hospital immediately. I knew by his voice something was very wrong. The only thing it could be was the baby.

Shurman and I drove our police car with the lights flashing.

The nurses' desk could not be seen. All the nurses and doctors were surrounding the desk. When we appeared, they all began to talk and talk loudly until Shurman yelled for them all to be quiet.

The doctor in charge said, "He's gone. The baby is gone."

He continued, "The baby ate and was checked out at six this morning. It was the next time we checked him when he was not in his crib. No one saw anyone enter the nursery."

It was very quiet as they all stared at Shurman and me. All we could do was stare at one another. Shock was settling into our bodies. We knew nothing about the mother or her family. Where she came from, her name, or where she was living. The baby was born on the street.

I did not want to cry. I was a policewoman. I was supposed to be strong but this was ripping me apart. Shurman put his arms around me. He was hurting. He wanted the baby as much as I did.

We asked each nurse what they could tell us. We asked each doctor caring for the baby in the nursery if they could have seen something that might not mean anything to them but we could use every detail to find this baby boy who was suppose to be ours.

Leaving the hospital without the baby was very hard on both of us. The hardest thing we ever had to do. We drove back to the police station to report and start our investigation, trying to find our baby.

We were told we should start the investigation, by asking for help whenever we needed it. Shurman and I drove home and took off our uniforms.

We were going to do our investigation in plain clothes. People tend to talk more freely to people in street clothes than uniforms.

We started by asking who saw the girl lay down on the street to have her baby. People were scared to talk about it, thinking it was so awful for the baby. No one seemed to know here and had not seen her around.

After talking to as many people as we could, someone said, "I saw a very well-dressed man talking to the girl earlier in the day and he looked angry."

Someone else said they had seen a big new car parked on the street that day. No one knew who the car belonged to. We talked to all the nearby store owners. The gas station attendant and to the local restaurant owners to see if the well-dressed man was in their stores. And did any of the workers talk to him. No one could help us but we couldn't give up.

We started all over again the next morning. This time we asked if the wealthy man was white or not.

No one could answer that either. It was getting more difficult each day. We had no real leads at all.

One man finally told Shurman a couple of numbers from the license plate on the big black car. We went directly to the police station and until midnight we went over every combination of numbers we could put together.

Suddenly Shurman said a man's name out loud. We immediately yelled, and every policeman helping us began searching and looking up his profile. Nothing was left unread.

We found the man was very wealthy. So, why was the girl homeless and why did she leave the baby? Why did the wealthy man come into town? Why was he looking for this homeless girl?

We knew now we had a lot of investigating to do. First, we had to find the wealthy man. Then, find out his connection to our baby. With the help of all of our friends affected by what had happened to us, they found the rich man's address. And his phone number.

I rang the phone number we found. The voice answered saying the owner was Mr. Warner, and that he was at his home in France.

Shurman turned his head and looked at me with a strange look on his face. I knew he was sad and disappointed.

I asked Shurman with tears in my eyes, "Do you think he took our baby boy to France? And why?" I felt as low as I could get.

As we drove back to the police station, we were both lost in our own thoughts. Then suddenly Shurman said, "Jo, how would you like to go to France?"

"I would love to," I answered with no doubt in my mind. The baby boy's bedroom was waiting for him.

I could not let Mr. Warner have our baby without a fierce fight. Shurman and I wanted this baby, more than anything in the world.

Chapter 8

This was a high priority crime case, and the entire police force was on board.

Our airline tickets were purchased. Schedules were made with the time difference in mind for our check-ins and the case.

It only took a few short minutes for both of us to finish packing. The ride to the airport was stressful. We wanted to tell each other how we were really feeling but we didn't want our fellow policeman, driving the car, to hear.

Once, on the plane and we were in our seats, we began to talk about how we were feeling.

We admitted we had never talked about having a baby of our own. This baby boy had come to us in a way that we could not understand. But, he meant so much to each of us in such a short time. The baby needed our help, to be cared for, and loved. We wanted to be there for him.

We both laid our heads back and drifted off to sleep. Our trip took nearly fourteen hours. We tried to rest as much as we could.

When the pilot's voice came over the loudspeaker and woke us both up, we listened to all of his information.

He suggested we could get a hotel room where we could find a good restaurant that served even better wine with our meal.

Shurman gave the name of the hotel the captain had mentioned to the taxi driver. He drove right to it. The restaurant was just a few blocks so we could walk to it easily.

The plan was to eat, then get a good night's rest in order to start looking for Mr. Warner the following day.

The emails and phone messages from our fellow officers will hopefully be helpful to find Mr. Warner. Nothing could stop us now.

The wine was so delicious with our meal. We each drank two full glasses of wine. Our hotel was so clean and warm. It was perfect for the desire that we were both feeling. Sleep came later after we made love. The sleep after was peaceful and calm. Not using protection was not on my mind. We were tired and stressed out, not knowing where our baby boy was.

Before I went to sleep, I thought about how far

Shurman had come on making love to me. He had changed completely. I always showed him I cared and loved him. His lovemaking became magical, and he made me feel wanted and needed.

Chapter 9

After we ordered breakfast through room service, we left for the nearest police station.

It didn't take long for the police to point on the map exactly where Mr. Warner lived. They all knew who he was. He lived in an exclusive,rich neighborhood. It was exactly what Shurman had thought. Mr. Warner was a very well-to-do man.

We drove a police car up to the large mansion, with a tall protective fence around it. Shurman turned off the engine, and we sat looking at each other for a moment. We both realized Mr. Warner was a well-known man.

The police department knew where he resided. They knew he was a man of means. You could not get into see him unless he was willing and wanted to see you.

The voice came loud and clear over the intercom at the security gate. With a thick French accent, he said, "You are to leave the area immediately." He had no idea who we were or what we wanted. We both knew he was told what to say.

Shurman started the car and turned it around, only driving a small distance. Then he pulled the car off of the road, just enough not to be seen if someone drove by.

Getting out of the car as quickly as we could, Shurman held onto my hand. He led me to the wall surrounding Mr. Warner's mansion. He put his hands together and lifted me up over the wall. He was tall and very strong. He pulled himself up and crawled over the high wall. I was waiting and hiding next to the wall.

Shurman found a window on the first floor he could raise up enough for me to slip through. My tiny body was inside. I reached back and slowly slid the window up enough for Shurman. But he could not get up and through the window. From the ground and up into the window was too far.

Looking directly in my eyes, he said, "Go!" I started into this huge mansion by myself. I had not worked alone before. Shurman was always by my side.

I slipped under the window. It was so dark. I went in feet first. My feet finally reached the floor as my hands were still holding onto the ledge. I let go, turned and reached into my vest for a flashlight.

The light told me I was in a bedroom. I made a quick search. It looked like a quiet bedroom. Ahead of me I saw a small light. Slowly I walked toward it, turning my flashlight off.

I found a large room with living room furniture and a beautiful fireplace with some small logs burning, giving off the small light. Ahead of me, I could see a room with a long table lined with vases each holding beautiful flowers. There were six lined up on each side of the table. I walked through the room, hoping the kitchen was close, and it was.

I turned my flashlight on and went into the kitchen. I walked up to the island and immediately spotted a large can. I put my flashlight on it and read exactly what was written on it. It was baby formula.

Suddenly, I felt I needed to see the baby's room. I left the kitchen and found winding steps leading upstairs. I took one step at a time as quietly as I could, hoping not to wake anyone up, including the baby.

Each door at the top of the steps was closed. The first door might be the master bedroom. So, I made a guess and opened the second door. It was meant for a baby, but, the baby was not there.

The baby bed stood in a blue-colored bedroom. The walls were all beautifully decorated. A closet was filled with baby boy clothes. The room was filled with all kinds of stuffed animals.

I turned my flashlight off and tiptoed to the steps. Reaching out and holding onto the banister, I took one step at a time. I used the same route to get back to the window. I pulled myself through the window, closed it and whispered Shurman's name. He was waiting for me. He lifted me up and over the tall fence. Then he pulled himself up and over.

We hurried to our car. We both opened and shut the car doors as quietly as possible. Shurman started the car and pulled onto the highway. We were on our way back to the police station.

All I could say was, "The baby has been here."

Chapter 10

I had taken all kinds of pictures while I was in each room, especially the baby's room. I also took a picture of the can of baby formula. In order to make a call, we have to have proof. I hoped my pictures turned out so the police could make a case.

The first thing Shurman asked the police captain was, "Does Mr. Warner have another house in France?"

The answer he received was, "Mr. Warner and his wife have a home in England."

I could feel Shurman's eyes on me. I realized at that moment we were going to England. I could feel Shurman telling me to get my bag without saying a word. We were on our way to the airport.

The captain continued, saying, "Your tickets will be waiting for you both at the airport."

With no hesitation, Shurman reached his hand out to me, pulling me toward the door.

Without any doubt in my mind, Shurman was going to find that baby boy. We both crawled into the police car. The ride was quiet as we sat holding hands, except for the occasional questions Shurman asked the driver.

He asked about Mr. Warner and his family. The driver told Shurman all he knew and had heard about the Warner family. He said, "The Warner family had a daughter and son. Nothing seemed to go right for the daughter. Talk around town was she hated her father. The son always tried to help her. He tried to protect her from their father and his abusive ways. The mother tried to help but her husband was stronger, and she always gave into him."

Chapter 11

Now we had all of this information to try and find out who gave birth to the baby boy. Why did Mr. Warner want the baby enough to take him out of the hospital and keep him hidden from everyone, including the police?

The bags were unloaded, and we headed for the ticket counter. It only took minutes and we were looking for our seats. When we were seated and in the air, we began to tell each other what our thoughts were.

Shurman was so determined to find the father,

mother, the Warner family and most of all, the baby boy.

We flagged down a taxi and asked to go to the closest police station. The driver looked a little alarmed. It was a very fast and quiet ride for all of us.

The driver jumped out, grabbed our bags, setting them on the street. He told us immediately the amount we owed and left the minute he received his money.

The police answered all of our questions and agreed to help us any way they could. Getting food and rest were what we both needed next. We ordered food brought to our room, and we slept all night so we could start again in the morning.

Shurman was up and dressed before me. After eating from the breakfast trays brought up to our room, we received a call. A police car was waiting for us out front.

The Warner home was in a small town outside of London. We asked the driver to pull off the road and wait for us. This time we got to the front door of the Warners' home. It looked as if a large fence was not permitted to be built around this smaller house.

Shurman knocked several times while I slipped around behind the small house, in case someone decided to leave by the back door.

A young woman opened the front door just enough so she could see Shurman standing there. She said, "There's no one home but me."

"Where's your parents and brother?" asked Shurman, trying to get the young girl to talk.

"They went out to eat," the young girl answered.

"Why didn't you go?" Shurman was trying hard to get her to say something that could be used against the family.

"I didn't want to," she answered. "I wasn't hungry."

Shurman was so determined, "Did they go for pizza?"

"No, they didn't have the baby. So, they went to the new restaurant in London," she said, realizing immediately that she had made a mistake mentioning the baby.

Now, we knew where the baby was. The baby was in the house, and the young girl was babysitting.

When I met up with Shurman again, I wanted to break down the door. I wanted to see the baby and hold him. But, Shurman took hold of my arm leading me to the police car.

Back at the police station, Shurman told the captain all that we had found out. He told him the baby is in Mr. Warner's house right now.

The captain thought a minute, then said, "I am going to send two different detectives to Mr. Warner's home and let them interview the family."

"Someone has to spend some time in jail for kidnapping the baby from the hospital in America," he continued. "You're too close for you both to do this. Your personal feelings would interfere."

As the captain looked directly at me, he said, "If you grabbed the baby, they would know why you are here to investigate and blame this all on you."

We both agreed to return to our hotel room and wait to hear from the captain. We knew we were too emotionally involved.

I went into the bathroom and slipped into a nice clean nightshirt. I laid down on the bed and covered up with a warm blanket. Shurman sat down on the edge of the bed next to me. He whispered, "Jo, I'd just like to hold you tonight."

I whispered back, saying, "Oh, Shurman, how I'd love that."

He lay down beside me, and I snuggled up against him. His strong arms pulled me closer to him. He whispered again in my ear, "I love you, Josephine." Within moments I heard his heavy breathing.

The ringing of the phone woke us up, and Shurman reached for it. The captain was calling us about what a couple of detectives had found.

The Warner house was empty. No one was there. Everything was gone, and there was no sign a baby had ever been there.

Our driver was outside waiting.

Chapter 12

We hurried to dress, and we did not talk on our trip to the station. The Warner family was always one step ahead of us. It was as if someone was warning them so they could get the baby moved before we got there. I was sure they wanted the baby. But, it must be so stressful on him not having his own familiar bed and surroundings.

The captain seemed more irritated than before. Shurman was very careful about what he said. He listened first and let the captain complain how difficult this search was. Then Shurman asked the captain if he would check every bus station, train station, airport in the area. He quickly added if the captain was short of help, we would do it right now. Shurman also asked to have police cars on the highway to stop any limousines driving out of town.

It took the captain a few minutes to decide, then he agreed to it. We both got up at the same time and headed right for the door. I was on my feet but I was not feeling as well as I wished I did. I was trying to keep up but Shurman was so determined to find the baby, he was suddenly five steps ahead of me.

We were able to use a police car for the trip to the bus station. There was no "Warner" listed on the passenger manifesto at the bus station. Then, onto check the trains leaving the city in the last seventy-two hours. Nothing.

We then arrived at the airport and found no "Warner" on the passenger list. We knew something was wrong. Shurman decided to get a hold of a phone book.

I began calling the list of Warners in the phone book. The first person hung up on me. We drove to their address. After finding the house, Shurman suggested I be the one to knock on the door.

An elderly man answered by opening the door only a crack. But as we talked, he told me about a Warner family living in the neighborhood whose daughter ran away. He thought she may have been pregnant. The hair on the back of my neck stood up. Was Mr. Warner's daughter the mother of the baby boy? Was she the girl who answered the door of the smaller house?

Shurman and I decided to talk to all of the neighbors again on either side of Mr. Warner's house. I took the house on the left.

The stories we both heard were nearly the same. The Warner family came to the house every year at this time to ski after a perfect snowstorm. Mr. Warner had a son and a daughter. The daughter was the oldest. She was the girl we had talked to.

Shurman and I now believed the baby belonged to Mr. Warner's daughter. But why was her father so determined to get the baby and keep it, even if he had to kidnap the baby?

The other two detectives also working on the case went to the school and talked to the principal about the Warner brother and sister. The story was long and painful for the entire Warner family. The girl, Jane Warner, was involved with a young man who came from a poor, uneducated family. Jane fell in love with him and was pregnant in her junior year in high school. Unfortunately, the young man was rude and treated Jane badly.

Mr. and Mrs. Warner would not let their daughter keep the baby. So, Jane stole enough money from her father to go to America and have the baby. She didn't want to go alone and bought a plane ticket for the boyfriend.

By the time they arrived in America, the couple was fighting terribly. Jane decided she was not going to keep the baby. She ran out of the hotel and suddenly the baby was coming. She just laid down on the street to have the baby.

Mr. Warner was on his way to rescue his daughter. He had no idea he was committing a crime by taking the baby from the hospital nursery. He flew his daughter and grandson to France first. Then all of the Warner family flew to England.

Shurman and I had all of the information we needed to find Mr. Warner and his family. Then a phone call changed everything. The phone call was from the principal of the high school the Warner children attended. He informed Shurman the father of Jane Warner's baby dropped out of school to find his baby.

He planned on caring and raising the baby himself. Although the young man had a lot of problems to deal with, his parents stated they could help raise the baby.

Now, the police department, Shurman and I, along with William G. Steinbeck, the father of the baby boy, were all looking for the missing baby.

The captain was told all the information about the Warner family, and he was not happy. He yelled, "We are going to have to start all over again!"

"Shurman and Josephine!" We heard our names called out so loudly, every policeman in the station heard him. "You both have to dig deeper. Someone knows something. Find out where Mr. Warner is hiding that baby boy."

Just as the captain stopped yelling, the police station door opened up, and Mr. Warner walked in, looking very upset and angry. No one said a word.

Finally, the captain asked, "Where do you have that baby hiding?"

"In an exasperated voice, Mr. Warner yelled back, "I don't have my grandson! He's been kidnapped by his no good father."

My heart was aching for that baby boy. He was torn from another home, and we could not find him.

Shurman and I sat Mr. Warner down at a table in a private room to interrogate him. After Mr. Warner began to talk, he seemed relieved to tell us all the misery he'd been through. We were aware of his story, starting when he took the baby from the hospital in America. His daughter was waiting for him in the hotel room. As soon as Mr. Warner brought the baby to the hotel, they left for France and their home.

Mr. Warner demanded his daughter take care of the baby. He insisted his daughter go to her senior year in high school while taking care of the baby when she returned home. Jane Warner's life would never be the same.

The captain asked Mr. Warner if Shurman and I could talk to Jane in case she could help find the baby. Jane knew William better than anyone else. She knew he had a temper that he couldn't control. She knew he had no money to buy the baby formula or diapers or clothing. My question to Jane was, "Does this bother you?"

Jane's answer, "Of course! William is not grown up. He has no job, and no way of finding one. If he is going to keep and take care of the baby, he'll need help."

"Then," I said, "you need to help us find William and the baby before something bad happens to your little boy."

Jane sat quiet for a few minutes, then said, "He could have gone to his grandmother's house. It's empty, and he has a key. He loved his grandma. She was always good to him."

"Jane," I said. "Tell us the address please."

After Jane told us, we left in a police care immediately. It took us an hour to get there. We pulled over by the neighbor's house so we would not scare him.

Shuirman went directly to the front door while I went around to the back of the house. Suddenly, the back door opened up. Shurman said, "He's not here now but he and the baby were definitely here."

I used my cell phone and called Jane Warner. I asked if she had any more information she could give us.

She said, "He always talked about living on a cattle ranch."

I asked, "Who would care for the baby?"

Her answer was, "That's how unstable he is."

"Who does he know on a farm?" I asked.

Jane said, "No one that he ever mentioned to me. You could ask his family."

After I begged her for a phone number, she gave me his mother's phone number. I let the phone ring quite a few times.

A man answered the phone. After identifying myself as the police, the man told me he was William's father. He said, "If you let him come home and let us help him raise his boy, I'll help. Otherwise, I'm hanging up."

"No," I said. "Let me talk to my captain. I know we can work something out. I'll call you right back."

I called the captain and told him everything that had happened.

"Captain," I said. "Please, let the young man bring the baby home to his family. Before something happens to the baby."

The captain was quiet on his end before finally speaking. He said, "Are you certain his father can get a hold of William to tell him to bring the baby home?"

Jane had been listening and nodded, "Yes."

I told the captain I was certain.

He said, "Call William's father back. Tell him there will be no charges brought against him if he brings the baby back unharmed. Today. Tell him the other grandparents, Mr. and Mrs. Warner, can help with the baby's care and expenses. If this does not work itself out soon, the adoptive parents will get to keep the baby."

My heart skipped a couple beats. Shurman reached over and took a hold of my hand. He wasn't giving up. He wanted the baby.

I looked at Jane. She sat with her head down while the captain was speaking. I said, "Jane, is there something you haven't told us?"

She looked up and said, "I just remembered something. William has an aunt and uncle living on a farm. I believe that's where he is heading with our baby."

Then she added, "I've never been there but I think I could find it."

With no hesitation, I relayed the information to the captain. In a strident voice he said, "What are you waiting for?"

Within minutes we were heading to the farm. Jane told Shurman what highway to take, and we were on our way. She also told him the farm was a long way off the highway. William had spent his summers there when he was twelve to fifteen years old. But his father and uncle had a falling out, and William no longer went to the farm.

Shurman and I took turns driving through the night. Keeping the gas tank full was important as the gas stations were many miles apart.

Jane woke just before dawn and informed us we were getting close. She directed Shurman down a long driveway and then up to the farmhouse. It was all lit up for morning breakfast.

Shurman walked to the door and talked to the aunt and uncle. The news was definitely not what we wanted to hear. They had not heard from William, and he was not there with the baby.

We were invited in for coffee and something to eat. We all walked slowly into the big farmhouse and sat down at the table for coffee. The trip was long. Shurman thought we should stay to see if William would show up later. We were invited to rest awhile to see if William came.

The police car was driven into a shed and the doors closed so no one could see it.

I immediately made a call to the captain and explained the situation. He didn't take it well but agreed to our staying in case William brought the baby there. Then the captain added, "If William isn't there by noon, you should start back to the police station. Take

Jane home. She needs to go back to school."

We waited until one o'clock before heading back. After the long drive back into the city and dropping Jane off at her home, we drove to the police station.

I had spent a lot of time questioning Jane during the car ride on all of the people William knew, and if there was someone else he would go to for help with the baby. Jane told us how surprised she was his family offered to help him as they never acted like they cared before.

She also stated, "How would he buy food? He never has had any money on him." She knew of no one else. No family that would help or take him in.

My stomach was upset, and it had been for days. Hearing this did not help at all.

The captain informed Shurman and I it was time to go back to the United States. The two other detectives would be continuing to search for William and the baby.

My stomach felt as if someone had punched me. But, this was not the time for me to talk about how I was feeling. The baby boy was what was important to us. He was out there somewhere, and it was up to Shurman and I to find him. Where could our baby be?

Chapter 13

Now, the captain was sending us home to the States. According to him, our work was done.

Shurman responded by saying to me, "I'm going to call home and ask our own captain if we could stay here and investigate on our own."

It was the answer Shurman had hoped for. Our captain said, "Stay as long as it takes to find that baby." We both breathed a sigh of relief.

"Let's go talk to William's friends. They might know something personal that they haven't told anyone else," I said to Shurman.

The first call we made was to Jane. She was very distant and cool talking to me. I tried to convince her my questions were meant only to help the baby. She mentioned William had very few friends that he talked to at school but told me two boys' names. When I thanked her, she said, "Billy will appreciate your caring," and hung up immediately.

I had never heard her call the baby by this name. I now suspected she had talked to William. I was sure she would deny it. After I told Shurman, he said, "Let's see what his two friends say and then we'll go after Jane."

Chapter 14

We didn't tell the captain here what our captain back home had said. We went directly to the hotel with a phone book, hoping to find the names and addresses of William's friends. We ordered a sandwich in. Eating a meal and getting rest was what we needed next.

The morning came so fast but we both knew we could not lose any time. The cab driver knew where everyone lived in this town. I wrote down all the streets we drove on.

The first boy was getting ready for school. We only had a few minutes to speak with him but he agreed to meet us after school. We would take him out for his evening meal. He explained he would have to ask his mother. We waited while he asked her. She thought it would be all right.

The two boys met with us, and we tried to make them comfortable so if they did know something, they would be okay to tell us. We had a nice meal together and at first, we talked about school and how each boy was doing and how they got along with William.

They both hesitated to say anything bad about William but each one admitted in a low-key voice that he was without too many friends. He just preferred to be alone.

Then I asked about William's baby. They both knew he was missing with the baby. The only thing they said that helped us was that they knew of William's family members who they thought would help him. They also said he had family in America. But, they did not know who they were or where they lived.

We thanked the boys and told them if either one heard from William, to please call us.

Shurman answered his phone, and it was Mr. Warner calling about the baby. Shurman understood Mr. Warner's need to know how his grandson was, and most of all if we knew the whereabouts of the baby.

He was still adamant about wanting to raise the baby. He told Shurman he could afford to take care of the baby, knowing William had no way to do it. Shurman's voice was calm and indicated to Mr. Warner he understood.

After hanging up, Shurman said, "We have to find Billy." I nodded my head and suddenly realized we were calling the baby by a name.

"Shurman, you called the baby by a name," I said. "Billy."

Shurman said, "Jane called him Billy." Shurman continued, "I think Jane has been talking to William. I think she knows where the baby and William are."

"We have to go back to the station," I told Shurman.

"Josephine, the captain wants us to go back to the States. Don't you remember? We can't go to the station. We need to go see Mr. Warner. He needs to tell us all the relatives he has because I'm thinking something is going on we don't know about. I think Jane has changed her mind and she wants her baby now."

Shurman was determined to find the baby.

We hailed a cab and gave the driver the address to the small house. No one answered the door. After walking the perimeter of the house and looking in all of the windows, we got back in the cab that had waited for us.

We gave the driver the address to Mr. Warner's mansion. Mr. Warner was kind enough to let us into talk about the baby. He did not at any time call the baby Billy.

Mr. Warner was pleasant and did not give out much information, stating, "I know of no one that would help William in his family."

Mr. Warner said, "Jane was back in school and doing well. She told me she would graduate in the spring."

He would not tell us more, saying, "I don't know anything else because Jane refuses to talk about William and the baby."

The only new information we learned was when he said, "I have an older sister living in America but she's too old to care for a baby."

Chapter 15

We directed the cab driver to take us back to the hotel and wait while we packed. It didn't take us long, and we were on our way to the airport. The first thing we did was check the passenger list.

The list had a father and baby, traveling to the United States but the name was not William Steinbeck. I immediately asked for the person on duty who had boarded them. The woman was willing to talk to us but she said, "The young mother was holding the baby the entire trip."

I then asked, "How old would you guess the baby was?"

She though a minute and said, "Maybe two months old."

I then asked about the mother. She answered saying, "Very young."

Shurman was listening. He suddenly looked mad. He said, "Mr. Warner lied to us about Jane."

The cab driver had left so we had to hail a different cab. We arrived at Mr. Warner's mansion, and he once again asked us in.

Shurman looked like he felt, and in a firm voice said, "Mr. Warner, you lied to us. Your daughter is on her way to America with your grandson and father of the baby."

"No! She's at school," he responded. "She said she'd be late tonight because she's staying at school for a play."

"Mr. Warner, you take us to the school, and we'll check on her," said Shurman.

The look on Mr. Warner's face told us he had believed what his daughter had told him.

We got back in the cab and drove to Jane's school. We went directly to the principal's office, and the principal informed us Jane had not been in class today. She went home because she was not feeling well. The room was so quiet. No one spoke. We all just stood and looked at each other.

I told Mr. Warner to give us his sister's address, along with anyone else he knew in America. He immediately did so.

Shurman explained to him we were going back to America that very night. He went on to say, "Mr. Warner, if we do find them, you and your wife should plan a trip to the United States."

I wanted this straightened up as soon as possible. I said, "Mr. Warner, we need to get this baby a home. Shurman and I have adoption papers signed, and we have hired a lawyer."

The look on Mr. Warner's face told me how surprised he was. Of course, he had no way of knowing we had done that while the baby was alone in the hospital, before he had taken the baby away.

"Mr. Warner, you might as well understand, you will not get this baby because you kidnapped him from the hospital. You will be arrested as soon as you get to America."

Mr Warner yelled, "Then I'm not going anywhere. I'm staying here right now."

Shurman responded to him by saying, "The police are watching you. If I were you, I'd go back to France as soon as possible."

Shurman continued, warning Mr. Warner to stop trying to get the baby. "You can just enjoy watching Billy grow up. You can see him as often as you want. I know you don't want William Steinbeck raising him. So, my wife and I will continue searching for him."

"I do not. I do not," Mr. Warner said with bitterness in his voice. Then he said, "I am going to leave with my wife right away. Please contact me at my home in France."

Chapter 16

Thinking about getting back on that huge airplane made my stomach even more upset. We boarded the plane and talked for a short period of time. Then we both went to sleep.

Arriving in New York in a rain storm made the decision to find a room and wait for the storm to be over easy.

After checking into a hotel, we both showered and went right to sleep for the night. In the morning we ate at a small cafe and went over all the addresses we had. We started by going to the closest one. It was Mr. Warner's sister's home. The destination was over an hour away.

The house was in a very nice gated community. I explained to the lady that opened the door who we were, how we knew her brother and why we were there. The lady was so excited to hear her brother, Vincent Warner, was doing all right, considering what he was going through with his daughter and the baby.

Gloria Benson explained to us, she had not heard from or seen William, Jane and their baby. I felt we had to make sure the baby had not been there. I asked to use her bathroom and headed for the kitchen. I found no signs of a baby there.

I returned to Shurman and nodded my head. We thanked Gloria Benson and left.

The next relative of Vincent Warner's on our list was a distant cousin living in a town nearly 100 hundred miles away.

We stopped along the way and ordered lunch at a restaurant. We asked all of the people working there if they had seen a young couple with a baby recently. No one was anxious to speak to us, not knowing who we were, or why we were asking about the couple. We thanked each one and left to find the distant cousin.

The address was in a neighborhood where most of the house needed repairs, especially fresh paint. The street had a lot of potholes needing asphalt. Old cars and pickups sat along side and behind the houses. No one was out on the street. I felt it wasn't safe to be outside in the area.

After finding the address, we parked in front of a neighbor's house. We both walked back to the right address. Shurman knocked. After a moment the door opened only enough to see a man's face. He asked, "What the hell do you want?"

Shurman remained as calm as he could. He then asked if he had see William, Jane and their baby.

The man was so defiant, answering, "Hell no."

I quickly started coughing over and over. I then pretended to choke and asked for a glass of water. He slammed the door. I opened the door behind him and followed him.

I thought he was going to hit me but I continued coughing and choking. I begged him for water. He turned, grabbed a dirty glass, filled it with water and handed it to me. I had just enough time to look around for any sign a baby had been there. The kitchen was so disgusting. Dirty dishes everywhere.

He pushed me to return to the door. I had not seen anything that led me to believe a baby had been there.

It was a relief to hand him the glass of water after not taking a drink from it. My coughing stopped and we left.

When we returned to the car, we did not say a word. Shurman leaned over and kissed me. I understood it was a relief to be leaving this area. Although we were disappointed we didn't find the baby, we were happy not finding the baby there.

We drove back the one hundred miles in the old car we had rented from the airport when we had arrived from England.

We had one more address to find when we got back to the city.

Vincent Warner had mentioned a friend he'd had for a very long time. He had talked about him in front of Jane. The man had moved to the United States after his daughter had married a soldier. He had taken her home to America to his family. The father could not stand to be so far away from his only daughter so he moved to the States.

We searched for the address most of the afternoon. It was in a middle class neighborhood. We parked down the street for a couple hours watching the house, in case we saw William or Jane entering or leaving.

After no one came to the house, we knocked on the door several times. A young woman opened the door, and I explained who we were looking for. She stated she had no idea who I was talking about. So I asked to use the bathroom in a hurry. She hesitated at first, then I acted like I really had to go. She told me where to find it. Instead I went to the kitchen and found nothing a baby would need: no formula, no bottles and no diapers in the garbage.

I hurried back to the door where Shurman was waiting for me. We both thanked the young woman and headed for our car.

After returning to our hotel room, we showered and laid down. It was only a matter of seconds before we were both asleep.

The morning came, and we were still sleeping. I woke up with the sun shining in my face. I woke Shurman. We both wanted breakfast, especially some coffee.

We sat in the restaurant trying to decide where we were going next. I was feeling like I needed more sleep. Something felt different with my body.

Shurman decided we needed to go back to our police station and start all over again. William and Jane were hiding their baby. Now, we had to do a lot of footwork. Who did they know in the States? We had to go back over everything.

We had just gotten started when a call came into the police station from a priest at the Holy Catholic Church on the west side of town. He sounded very upset. A person had left a newborn baby in a cardboard box on the steps of the church.

We both jumped up and excitedly told our captain we would take care of it. We both thought we had found the baby boy who was going to be ours.

We took the first police car parked outside. With the lights flashing and the speed we were going, traffic pulled over for us. We arrived to find the priest and several nuns near the altar. The priest was holding the baby. We both looked at the baby, then at each other. I said, "We have come for the baby. We have to take him to the hospital to be checked by a doctor."

After a collective outburst, one of the nuns said, "It is not a him. It's a girl." Shurman yelled, "Are you sure?" When they were all done laughing at him, they agreed, "We are sure."

I held the baby on the way to the hospital, and I just wanted to keep holding her. I later called our lawyer and explained everything. He stated he'd start the paperwork.

I thought about the blue room we had waiting at our home. So I called my parents, knowing if I asked, the extra bedroom in our home would be painted pink before we could bring her home.

The baby girl did not have anything on her to look for identification. The clothes she had on had been washed quite a few times. We had nothing. We did not know if she even had a name.

The girl weighed seven lbs. six ounces. She was nineteen inches long. Everything about her body was perfect. The nurses all loved her immediately. The doctor who cared for her treated her like one of his own children.

We were aware the paperwork would take at least two weeks. The nurses had to find a formula she liked and agreed with her. They had bathed and changed her clothes. I held her to feed her a bottle. It was unknown if her birth mother had fed her at all. The baby caught on to suck the bottle. She took two ounces of milk and went to sleep. I sat holding her and thinking how easy it would be to love her as her mother.

The nurse took the baby girl and laid her in a bassinet. I left the hospital with Shurman feeling sad, not knowing if we would get one of the babies.

Chapter 17

We drove home to get some rest and talk over our next move in finding William, Jane and Billy.

Shurman called Mr. Warner, father of Jane and grandfather of Billy. He asked Mr. Warner if he had heard from his daughter, Jane.

Mr. Warner answered saying he had not heard from her. He told Shurman how upset he was over William taking his daughter and his baby grandson so far away to America.

Shurman asked him again if he knew of anyone else the young couple could be staying with. Mr. Warner said, "Have you checked the shelters you have in America?"

Shurman told him, "No, but we will go as soon as we finish breakfast.

I was still eating when Shurman started to get up. I simply said, "I'll be done in a minute." Lately, my stomach was either feeling upset, or I was very hungry. This morning I felt hungry, and I needed to eat.

The first shelter we found in the phone book was only a short distance away. The building needed repair but once inside, it was well-cared for. The ladies we talked to were polite and knew every person who had stayed there that whole week. They also went on to say if we wanted the resident list for last month, they could look it up for us.

We checked every name, and we were sure William, Jane and the baby had not stayed there. We left for the address of the next shelter. It was a short drive into the next town.

The shelter looked well-cared for. After finding the same thing that William, Jane and the baby hadn't stayed there, we drove back to the police station. We sent a message out to as many shelters as we could. with the names and descriptions of the young couple and baby.

The answers we received back were all the same. No one fitting the description of the couple with a baby were seen at any of the shelters we had sent a message to.

It suddenly occurred to me it was possible, we would never find the baby. Shurman was busy on the police department's computer reaching out to every city in the state, asking for help finding the couple and baby. He gave every bit of information we had.

The answers always came back the same. No one

fitting their description was seen. But the shelters will be on the look out for the couple and baby.

Needless to say we were so disappointed. Shurman mentioned he had another idea. We would check the orphanages. He went on to say, "What if they ran out of money and had to give Billy up?"

I put my head down and began to cry. Shurman put his arms around me and said, "We have a better chance of getting him as our own if this would happen."

All I could say while I cried was,"Poor Billy, what a life he has had so far."

Shurman sent word again, "Needing Help" to every orphanage in the area. He also contacted orphanages in the nearby states, expanding our search.

I woke to our phone ringing. The voice on the other end sounded excited, telling me that Shurman and I should come to the nursery in the hospital.

It took a short time, and we hurried into the very busy hospital. We were walking down the hall to the office of the nursery when we saw the nurse in charge, along with the doctor who cared for the baby girl we had brought in from the church.

The nurse walked directly up to me and placed the baby girl in my arms. The tears ran down my cheeks. Shurman wiped my eyes with the biggest smile on his face, then said, "I think we have a baby girl."

"Yes," the doctor said. "You have been approved to adopt the baby." I immediately asked if I could sit down.

My whole body felt weak. My stomach felt nervous. I did not want to throw up while holding this beautiful baby girl. Shurman stood quietly waiting to hold her. I stood and gently placed her in his arms. The nurses gave me all the instructions for feeding her and caring for her. My mother and father were at our home waiting for us.

We drove home and placed her in her new crib. She was completely relaxed while Shurman and I were tense and shaking over the new responsibility of this tiny human being.

Chapter 18

Shurman left for the police station. He needed to tell the captain our story. He needed to tell him I would be on maternity leave for a few months, and he would need a new partner to replace me.

The captain was mad but also happy for us. He mentioned two men who could replace me. Shurman was willing to accept either one. Once the decision was made, he and Shurman started searching together.

They visited and questioned every orphanage in the area. The orphanages in other states were checked over the internet and calls on the police radio were made all day.

It was a day later when a report came over the police radio saying in a city three states away a little baby had been left after the parents had spent a week in the shelter close to the orphanage. They were out of money. They could not buy formula for their baby. They came to the orphanage and left the baby with no identification.

The excitement in the station was palpable. Shurman and his new partner headed for the airport for tickets to fly to the city that sent the new message. They boarded the first airplane going into the city where the orphanage was.

Shurman called me from the airport and explained what was happening. First, I couldn't believe it. Then I cried happy tears. I told Shurman we needed to think of a name for our baby girl. He answered saying, "I have been thinking of one." Shurman said, "Myra Christine."

I squealed with happiness. It was perfect for this perfect little girl that we both loved so much. I could hear his familiar little giggle. His joy showed all over his face when he came home that night. He sat and held her, talking to her while he fed her. After the bottle was finished and she went to sleep, he placed her gently down in her crib.

Myra Christine belonged to us, now and forever.

Chapter 19

The ride on the airplane for Shurman and his partner was uneventful. They both dozed off and rested a bit. Renting a car took longer than usual. But, it gave them time to find the directions to the orphanage. After proving who they were and asking to see the baby, they were told it was a baby boy. They were also told the couple who left him was young. Because they no longer could buy formula or anything else to care for him, they had no other choice.

The couple refused to give any names. But, the nurse remembered the mother slipped once and called the baby, Billy, before they left. Shurman fought tears back and turned around so no one could see his face. He had found Billy.

Sheurman and his partner asked the orphanage to fly Billy, along with a nurse to help care for him back to our hometown and to the hospital were Billy was born.

Shurman then called his captain at the police station. He asked if the department would pay for the cost of flying Billy, a nurse and his partner home. After the captain asked what the cost would be, he talked it over with his secretary and agreed to do it.

The hospital staff was all surprised to see how well Billy looked. He was a happy baby. Everyone wanted to know what was going to happen to him. Shurman told the entire staff, Billy belonged to him and Josephine. The adoption papers were in their lawyer's office.

After Billy was there two days, the lawyer delivered the adoption papers. Everything was all in order for Billy to be dismissed to Shurman and me.

The party in the nursery when Shurman picked up our son to take him home brought a lot of tears to every nurse and doctor on duty.

I complained of not feeling well earlier that morning so I stayed and waited for Shurman to bring Billy home.

Shurman knocked on our front door, and I opened it to see Shurman carrying our new son, and he handed Billy to me. I held open my arms. I deeply loved him.

Chapter 20

Messages were sent to Mr. and Mrs. Warner about their grandson and the adoption. Mr. Warner was asked to find his daughter and inform her that Billy has a new home forever. If his family wanted to see him, everyone is welcome.

Two high chairs sat in the kitchen for the two babies. I was so happy with my family. My parents came each day and were overjoyed to be able to help.

Shurman went back to work after a few days while

I stayed home on maternity leave. Shurman insisted I go see a doctor. My parents were wiling to stay with Myra and Billy.

The doctor scolded me for not taking better care of myself. I told the doctor what had happened lately and about Billy and Myra.

After all the tests were done, the doctor sat at his desk and drew in a deep breath. He had such a strange look on his face. He began by telling me I was healthy but I definitely needed more rest.

"Now, Josephine, I have one more thing to tell you." My eyes widened waiting for the doctor to tell me.

"Josephine, you are three months pregnant."

No words could come out of my mouth. The doctor and I sat looking at each other in stunned silence. I finally mustered, "Doctor, are you sure?"

The doctor replied, "I'm going to show you a picture of your baby." After the ultrasound was completed, and I saw the baby, I was thrilled beyond measure. Nothing could have made me happier.

I sank into my car and sat a minute. How was I going to tell Shurman? I was nearby home when I made the decision to wait a few days to tell Shurman about his baby on the way. I thought for now I should let him and his new partner solve their case. He needed to get some rest, too, as he had been up early each morning and late getting home each night.

Billy and Myra loved his gentle loving care. Shurman came home once in a while early enough to play with them and read to them. He helped get them ready for bed and held them to give each one their nighttime bottle.

Early in the morning Shurman was ready to pick up his partner and proceed to the police station, hoping to get his new case solved.

Shurman told me about the young couple who had been breaking into jewelry stores, loan shops and pawn shops. The shops were located in small towns many miles apart

Each town was complaining about the amount of money they were losing. Then, the young couple suddenly stopped breaking into any more shops. Everything was very quiet.

The couple had dressed differently for each break-in so no one could identify them. The money was gone. The young couple was gone.

Shurman and his partner had very few clues to go on. Shurman came home and explained to me how his day was spent, interviewing all of the shop owners.. Each one told a different story on who they thought got all of their money. The robbers left no fingerprints or any evidence behind in the stores.

After Shurman played with the babies and helped put them to bed, I said to him, "It has to be a couple that really needed money for something specific. Maybe they planned on using the money to pay back someone or some company or keeping someone for them."

Shurman jumped up and said, "Yes! Yes! I'm going to see the captain. I'll pickup John on the way. We are going up to the shelter. We will be gone all night."

Shurman put his arms around me and kissed me. He whispered, "Thank you."

I checked on Billy and Myra. For the time being we had both of them in Billy's room. It was just easier that way. I leaned down and kissed them before leaving, closed the door. For some reason goosebumps ran down my arms and legs.

Then, I heard a knock on our door. I hesitated. The knock got louder. I grabbed my phone and speed-dialed Shurman. He didn't answer. I texted him, "911."

I heard someone yell, "Open up!"

I didn't want to do it. I ran back into our bedroom and to my middle drawer in the closet. I lifted up an extra blanket to get my gun safe. I turned the combination lock as fast as I could. I picked up my gun, tucked it into my belt and pulled down my sweatshirt over my jeans.

I got back to the door and with my hand shaking, I placed my hand around the doorknob, then I heard a male voice say, "Open this damn door or else."

Trying to stall for time, hoping Shurman would come home, I asked, "Who is it?" There was no answer for a few minutes. Then the voice said, "I just want to talk to you."

I answered by asking, "What is this regarding?"

I could hear whispering on the other side of the door. Finally, a female voice simply said, "Please."

I didn't want this to wake up the babies so I opened the door. I had seen them both before. It was William and Jane.

Chapter 21

William immediately walked right up to me. He was only a few inches from my face and said, "Where is my son?" I could hardly get my breath. He kept getting closer to my face.

He yelled to Jane while scanning the whole room. "Jane, go look for Billy and bring him out here. We're taking him with us."

I was frantic! I said, in a nervous, scared voice, "No. He's asleep. You can't take him. We adopted him. I have papers to prove it."

He yelled back in my face, "He's my son. You can't just take someone's son and adopt him."

Just as I was going to scream at him, Shurman and his partner walked through the door. The relief I felt was indescribable.

Jane came out of the babies' bedroom, carrying Billy. Billy was half asleep, starting to wake up and moving around in her arms. Billy had no idea what was going on. He opened his eyes and didn't know who Jane was. He started to fuss and cry. I walked up to Jane and took Billy from her forcefully. I pressed him to my chest like I always do. He settled down, relaxed and closed his eyes.

Shurman stood firmly in front of the door. No one was taking our baby boy out of our house.

William took a step toward me. Shurman's partner stepped up in front of William and stopped him. Shurman loudly said, "You both need to leave and bring your lawyer with you to the police station."

I gently laid Billy back in his bed. He hardly moved. He closed his eyes and went back to sleep. Loving him was so easy, and my heart was so heavy for Jane. Being a mother and then a sudden change had taken the baby from you. How does a mother stand it? Having that small warm body taken from your arms and heart?

My next thought was to call Jane's father in France and explain what has happened, and remind him that Shurman and I are raising his grandson in America. We legally adopted Billy.

I explained to Shurman what I had decided to do. Shurman replied that he would talk to Mr. Warner also. I let Shurman have my phone after I rang Mr. Warner's phone number. I could hear Mr. Warner answer his phone.

Shurman talked softly at first. Then when Shurman had explained all the details, the conversation got very loud and heated. I gently took the phone away from Shurman's ear and out of his hand.

I told Mr. Warner his grandson was in a very loving home and would be raised by a loving mother and father. I also told him he could call whenever he wanted to. His anger continued. He stated he would be here in two days and that he was not leaving without Billy. I ended the conversation as sincerely as I could, hoping to calm him down.

Shurman left the room and walked into the babies' room to check on both of them. He returned and walked up to me. He put his arms around me and kissed me while holding me tightly against him.

He whispered in my ear, "Mr. Warner is not getting Billy. He belongs with us." I stood very still but the baby inside me was moving. I was sure now. There was no denying it. I had no choice but to tell Shurman soon. The time now did not appear to be just right.

Chapter 22

Two days slipped by so fast. I had just put the babies down to nap when I heard the doorbell ring continuously.

I quickly grabbed my phone and texted "911" to Shurman. I slowly opened the door, knowing exactly who was on the other side.

Mr. Warner and his wife stood holding a baby sling.

They came to take their grandson home to France. My body felt as if it would slip to the floor at any minute but I could not let that happen.

The Warners walked right up to me and stood as close as they could get. Mr. Warner spoke first. He looked directly into my eyes and said, "Get my grandson now." Everything I had learned in police training kicked in.

I put my shoulders back, saying simply and firmly, "No." It was a shock to him. But it shocked me a lot more. Billy was not going with the Warners. Billy was not leaving Shurman's and my home.

The adoption papers were signed. Billy belonged to us. I was beginning to feel desperate. I had no idea what to say or do next.

Shurman's car lights flashed across the front of our house. My racing heart slowed down a bit seeing them. He was inside the house within seconds.

Looking directly at Mr. Warner, in a voice that gave me chills, Shurman said, "Leave my house now."

Mr. Warner answered saying, "I'm coming back for my grandson."

After the couple was gone, Shruman said, "Dress the babies warmly. We need to take them somewhere they'll be safe. We can take them to Grandpa's house. No one will find us there."

A picture of the house immediately came into my mind. No one had lived in it for nearly five years. It had not been used, let alone cleaned that entire time.

I wanted to tell him no but Shurman was right. No one would look for us there.

Shurman added, "My partner, John, will stay here. I'll go to the police station and go see our lawyer."

We put both babies in their car seats and started out of town. The hour went so fast. We pulled into the driveway which had weeds growing everywhere. The house looked truly abandoned.

Chapter 23

The situation had changed. We were now the hunted.

We carried the babies into the house. The first thing we did was go to the bedroom. While I held both of the babies, Shurman pulled the mattress off of the bed and laid it on the floor. He stripped the bed, and I gently placed the babies down on the mattress. Then it all hit us.

The smell in the house was horrific. There were spider webs everywhere. All the rooms were filled with clutter and garbage. I walked into the kitchen and could hardly comprehend what I saw before me. There were dirty dishes on every surface available including the window sills. All the plates, bowls, cups and silverware had been used but never cleaned or put away.

The floor was so sticky and dirty, my shoes stuck each step I took. The stove top had pans with dried up food still in them. There were opened cans of peaches left on the table along with hardened bread crusts and egg shells. The odor gagged me.

I'm sure Shurman's grandma would have never left her house looking the way it did now.

The dining room and living room were also in disarray. Newspapers were spread out everywhere on the furniture and on the floor.

Suddenly I heard angry voices. I knew one of them was Shurman. I ran into the bedroom where the babies were. They were fine. Then I heard Shurman yelling, "Get up and out of my house." Coming down the hall, being pushed along by Shurman was a man wearing worn-out pants and a dirty shirt. His stringy hair and whiskers were gray.

I stepped in the babies' room while Shurman escorted the man and his belongings out of the house. I heard Shurman warn him he must never come here again.

I had a bad feeling this was only the beginning of dealing with this homeless man.

I began filling garbage bags with all the newspapers, cans and trash. I lined them up across the dining room and into the living room. I deep-cleaned the kitchen sink and counter top so I could mix the babies' bottles of formula. All the while, I felt nauseated, gagging at the intense smells.

I finally gave in and laid down next to the babies Shurman had placed pillows completely around the edge of the mattress so the babies did not fall off.

I suddenly jerked awake, hearing footsteps outside the bedroom door. I knew the outside doors were locked so it had to be Shurman. I waited a few moments for Shurman to come in but he didn't.

I opened the door slowly, looked down the hall as the last bedroom door was closing. The man was back, and he was in the house.

I texted "911" to Shurman, hoping he'd come immediately. I heard more footsteps out in the hall. I was extremely happy. Shurman was here. I waited for the bedroom door to open and to see his face.

Suddenly, the door swung open and a man wearing a long filthy coat, covered in God knows what, was looking back at me. The smell was so pungent I started to gag again.

He yelled, "What are you doing here?"

"My husband happens to own this house," I replied. "His grandparents left it to him. He was in college and then he was enrolled in the police academy. If I were you, I'd start packing and also tell all your buddies to pack, too, or he'll have you all arrested." I shut the door in his face.

I again heard footsteps head down the hall to the last bedroom where the door opened and shut loudly. Then I heard the door open again and two sets of boots were running toward the front of the house that leads outside. I couldn't help but think they were going to look for a new place to squat.

Chapter 24

The bedroom door opened, and Shurman walked in. He looked angry and stressed out. He came directly to me, pulled me in close and wrapped me in his arms. He kissed me like he did the night we were married over and over. I held him while his body was shaking.

I knew something was very wrong. He finally said, "Mr. Warner called me. His lawyer informed him a decision by the judge would be made within a month as to who will raise Billy. Mr. Warner is planning to stay in America so when the judge makes the decision to let the baby's birth family have him, he'll take Billy back to France immediately."

Shurman's voice was trembling by the time he was through telling me. I did not let him go until he finished speaking. He finally calmed down and stopped shaking. I softly kissed him and whispered, "It's all going to work out as it should, Shurman."

We both decided cleaning up the house would keep us very busy until we heard from the judge that was handling our case.

I made the difficult decision to keep my secret until

we found out about where Billy's home would be.

The following week we were both busy. Shurman worked his job while I cared for the babies. We worked together on the home. Every door and window was replaced. There were new locks put on. We also installed cameras over each door. With the new locks, the squatters could not get in. The babies would be safe, especially whenever Shurman worked at night, and I would be alone with them.

We had to wait one more week for the judge's answer. We didn't talk about it. It was too hard and difficult for both of us. Giving up Billy would stress us both out. Also, I felt I had to wait a little longer to tell Shurman about the baby I was carrying. But I couldn't keep the secret much longer. My body was changing and my stomach growing.

My doctor called and insisted I come to the office for vitamins. I could not ask Shurman to watch the babies so I took them both with me. It was like caring for twins. The babies are nearly the same age, only a month apart. I made sure I could get home before Shurman did. I was exhausted.

I called the nearest restaurant and ordered a complete evening meal to be delivered. Shurman came home with no news. The judge had not decided yet.

I kept going over in my mind something the doctor had said to me about how I was growing so fast. I knew I couldn't keep the secret much longer from Shurman. We were both under so much stress. The time never seemed right.

Shurman called me. His voice sounded a mix between upset and angry. He said, "The judge sent a message to us. He asked for all the parties associated with baby Billy's adoption lawsuit to meet at the courthouse in two days at 10 a.m., Wednesday morning, second floor in Room 200."

I told Shurman I would call and ask my parents to come and watch the babies.

"No," Shurman said. "We have to take Billy with us. They will only have to watch Myra."

I was listening and trying to understand why we had to take Billy. Then it dawned on me, how it was possible Billy might not be coming home with us.

Chapter 25

Shurman called from work, he said, "I love you, Jo." And then hung up. I found the nearest chair and quickly sat down. I was thinking now might be the right time to tell Shurman about our baby on the way. I had two days to decide.

The two days finally passed. I waited until the last minute but I knew I had to dress Billy, take along a change of clothes, formula, two full bottles, along with his diapers. As I packed his possessions, I had to stop and wipe the tears from my eyes to see what I was doing. The sad tears would not stop.

My parents arrived to watch Myra. Shurman came into the house without saying a word and picked up Billy while I carried the rest.

We rode in a police car to the courthouse and did not talk. We took the steps up to the second floor and entered the room where Mr. Warner, his wife, William and Jane were sitting with their lawyer.

The room felt cold. Billy had gone to sleep in Shurman's arms. I covered Billy so they could not see him. I was getting angry.

We all stood when the judge came into the room. He began talking about families, specifically, blood families. At that point, I was sure Billy would not be going home to our house. He would be going home with his birth family, and our adoption papers would be null and void.

The judge was getting closer to the end of his speech when he said, "I have decided Billy should be returned to his blood family."

The judge went on to say, "Shurman and Josephine, Mr. Warner has informed me he and his wife have bought a house in America, right here in this city. When the family is here in America, you are allowed to visit Billy. Mr. Warner and the family thinks you have cared for Billy better than anyone else ever could.

He stood up and left the room, and two officers came in. One of them walked directly up to Shurman and reached his arms out for Shurman to place Billy in his arms. Shurman uncovered Billy so we could kiss him goodbye. The sadness I felt was indescribable. I took a quick look at Shurman. He also had tears in his eyes as he kissed Billy and laid him in the officer's arms.

The officer in turn, placed Billy in Jane's arms while William stood on one side of her and her parents on the other side.

Shurman and I left the courthouse, holding tightly to each other. That night we laid in bed with our arms around each other after putting Myra to bed.

The following morning I slipped out of bed as not to waken Shurman. I prepared his favorite breakfast. I had decided to tell Shurman about the baby I was carrying.

We both sat down at the breakfast table. With looks of sadness on our faces, neither one of us was talking. Finally, I said, "I have something to tell you."

I stood up and walked over to him. I put my arms around his shoulders and said, "I"m going to have a baby.

That's all I needed to say. The look on his face changed. He began smiling from ear to ear. He grabbed me and sat me down on his lap.

He said, "I couldn't be happier."

I couldn't have loved him more in that moment. I felt so much emotion over our baby, and tremendous relief all through my body.

We finished breakfast as we talked about our baby on the way and how excited we were for Myra to have a sibling. We're so grateful for the new blessing and to have a beautiful home to bring up our baby and Myra in.

Chapter 26

The months I had left slipped by, and our baby boy was born in the spring. The joy and the love we felt for him filled up our lives.

The day we received the letter was an ordinary day. Shurman went to work, and I took care of the children. I looked at the return address. It was from a law office with a lawyer's name we did not know, from a city we were not aware of.

I slowly opened the letter and began to read. I only read a few lines and had to sit down. It started by saying the mother of the baby girl that was left on the Holy Catholic Church steps wanted her baby.

I immediately became ill. I texted Shurman and asked if he could come home. Nothing made any sense. Myra was two years old.

I heard the door open, and Shurman's footsteps hurrying into the kitchen. I was sitting at the table with the letter laying in front of me. He sat down beside me, picked up the letter and began reading it.

His demeanor changed instantly.

Shurman read the letter several times, then stood up and kissed me on the forehead. He said, "Jo, I'm going back to the police station and look up all I can about this law office, this lawyer and the woman who left Myra on the church steps. Then, I'll go to our lawyer's. I'll be back as soon as I have some news."

Myra and our son, Ross, ate their lunch and I put them both down for their naps. I waited impatiently for Shurman. It was nearly dark when he returned with news.

He walked into our house and took my hands and sat me down to tell me. The woman claiming the right to our baby girl, who gave birth to Myra, works in this law office. She is actually getting married to the attorney working on the case.

Our lawyer said, "We may have a big fight ahead of us."

Sobbing, I said, "I'm begging you, Shurman. Don't let them take my little girl away from me."

"I promise I will do everything I can for us to keep Myra as our own," Shurman said, with his voice shaking. He went on to say, he was going back to the station to do more investigating to see if the woman had a police record so he could report it to our lawyer.

Myra woke up wanting to play with Ross. They had no idea the awful situation we were in. Our family could be split up again.

Shurman gathered all the information he could,-

from the clothes Myra was wearing the day she was dropped off on the steps of the church to the cardboard box she was found in. There was no formula or bottles left with her.

Shurman was going over every little detail. He searched the hospital records and wrote down the condition of Myra's skin and also how hungry she acted. He even tried to find where the cardboard box came from, and if it had a name on the side of it.

Shurman made one more call to me to ask if I could remember anything else, the smallest little detail. I mentioned Myra needed a bath when we got her from the church. I again went over all the information, and Shurman was sure he had it all. He was on his way to our lawyer's office to have our lawyer send a professional letter to the woman's lawyer.

Chapter 27

Our lawyer explained to Shurman the letter would be sent the following day. He went on to say, "I'm sure we'll hear from him in two days. I will call you the minute I hear anything."

Over the next two days I tried to keep busy with the babies while I was feeling a little bit tired and my stomach was queasy.

The lawyer's office called to make an appointment

with us to come in and talk about the letter he received.

Myra took such good care of Ross, always made sure he had a toy to play with, made sure he was warm. She always helped feed him. I cried more the next two days than I had since losing Billy.

My parents came to care for Myra and Ross when we dressed to go to the lawyer's office. I couldn't lose her. I just couldn't.

As we parked our car in front of the lawyer's office, Shurman said, "Please, Jo. You have been such a loving mother to Myra. Now lean on me."

I knew then he believed we would lose her to a mother that had given Myra away.

We walked into the office, and the room was so cold. The chair I sat in was cold. Our lawyer greeted us warmly and began by saying, "I received a letter personally from your baby girl's mother."

Right then, tears welled up in my eyes and rolled down my cheeks. I couldn't stop them. I felt Myra's arms around my neck. I could her yelling, "No, Mama. No."

The letter began with the mother writing, "Thank you both for the care and love you have given my little girl. My fiance and I feel you are fighting so hard to keep her because you both love her very much. With a sad heart, I am not going to try and take her away from you. I would some day like to see and meet her."

My whole world exploded! I heard music. I saw

fireworks. I leapt out of my chair, threw my arms around Shurman and kissed him.

His arms held me so tight I couldn't move. The lawyer jumped up and threw his arms around both of us. At that moment we lowered our heads and said our own silent prayer to God.

I rode home in the police car. I sat as close to Shurman as I could. My mind was going over every word in the letter. It had to be so very hard for Myra's birth mother to give her up. But, Myra belongs to Shurman and I, now and forever.

The following morning our life went back to normal. Shurman left for work, and I took care of our family that we both loved so very much.

I made an appointment to see the doctor. He confirmed my pregnancy. Shurman was the first to know. He was so happy. Nothing could have pleased him more.

Chapter 28

Our life couldn't have been better. Shurman told me about the case he was working on with his partner, and I listened. I was concerned but not worried.

After Shurman left for work, he called me. He said, "Something is going on at the Warners' new home here. As soon as I find out, I'll call."

My body began to tremble. My first thought was the safety of Billy. The afternoon went by slowly. I did my usual care of Myra and Ross. Then I prepared our evening meal.

I did my evening care of the children and gave them a snack before putting them to bed for the night. I still had not heard from Shurman, and it was now dark out. Instead of going to bed, I decided to wait up for Shurman to tell him what the children had done that day.

It was nearly midnight and suddenly, the doorbell rang. I jumped up out of my chair, nearly running to the door with all the fear I felt racing through my body. I put my hand on the knob to open the door. I was so frightened.

The first thing I saw were dark blue uniforms, which I knew instantly meant that I was going to receive very bad news.

The first words I heard the officer say was, "I'm sorry to tell you--"

"I yelled, No. Do not tell me that!"

He quickly said, "No. Shurman is alive. He is in the hospital but he has been shot. We're here to take you to the hospital."

I made a call to my parents. I was not allowed to drive myself so after they arrived, I crawled into the police car. It took only a short time, and we were there.

The bullet entered above his heart, missing the heart muscle itself. Thankfully, the gunshot did not do a lot of damage. Shurman was in surgery when I arrived. They assured me at the desk, Shurman would survive.

Nothing made any sense to me at two o'clock in the morning. I remembered Shurman telling me there was a disturbance at the Warner residence.

While I waited, I called Shurman's partner, John. He had all the information on the terrible shooting that had taken place.

William had stayed out all night with a gang he was affiliated with. They had done a lot of drugs and ended up fighting. William had made it home but he was carrying a gun. William got a little loud.

Mrs. Warner, knowing Shurman was a policeman, called him and asked if he would come to the house.

Shurman and his partner got to the house and heard gunshots. When they entered the house, they saw both Mr. and Mrs. Warner lying on the floor. William was standing over them. When he turned the gun on Shurman, John shot back and wounded William badly.

William ended up in the hospital, down the hall from Shurman with a policeman guarding the door to his room. He would be arrested for the murder of Mr. and Mrs. Warner.

I continually asked about Billy. No one seemed to know. I decided to go to the house and speak directly with Jane.

The police surrounded the house. I had to show

them my ID to get in. After knocking at the door several times, Jane opened the door a small crack. She looked disappointed when she saw me but she let me in.

Jane looked like she had not slept for several nights. Her eyes were nearly swollen shut. She was at her lowest. She could not stop sobbing while she was trying to talk. She was only eighteen, and her whole world had come crushing down on her.

She stated how alone she was and how was she going to care for Billy while she was in school and also the years of college. Her father had insisted she go to college.

Jane was holding Billy while he was crying and fussing in her arms. I reached for him, and she handed him to me. He felt so familiar in my arms. He cuddled up and laid his head on my shoulder and went to sleep, just like he had always done. He always cuddled up against my chest.

The next two weeks I spent my time with Shurman in his hospital room. He was being dismissed in a couple of days. He was giving the nurses and doctors a hard time because he was ready to go home and back to work.

Myra and Ross were so happy to see him. They would not leave him alone for one minute. My body continued to change and grow. Shurman helped me as much as he could.

The day finally came when the doctor told him he

could work half days but Shurman did not know what half days were. He would leave early in the morning and come home late at night.

I tried to stay up and wait until he came home at night but my days were also long. I could not stay awake. Both of the children got up early and always needed my attention.

It was the middle of the morning and the doorbell rang. Before I could get to the door, it rang again. I quickly opened the door to find Jane standing there.

It had been three weeks since the terrible tragedy. She stood holding Billy. Beside her was a large suitcase. Her eyes were all red. I immediately invited her in. Jane stepped in and tried to tell me what she was doing here.

She said, "I can't do this anymore. I have been taking Billy with me to class. I'm giving him to you to raise. I promise I will not take him away from you."

I was hearing her words but this was so much to take in after losing him once before.

Jane went on to say, "He must be told I am his mother, and I did this because I love him." She stepped out and brought the suitcase in and left my home.

After my call, Shurman came right home. He was in disbelief as much as I was. Nothing could have surprised us more.

Shurman sat holding Billy, playing with him for a long time. It was just like before we had to give him up. It was as if nothing had changed. Billy walked through the house remembering.

Our biggest fear was Jane returning and wanting Billy back as soon as she graduated from high school. Each day we woke wondering if this was the day.

Shurman notified our lawyer with every detail. A letter was hand delivered to Jane by our lawyer to sign. The lawyer assured Shurman Jane understood. He went on to say the Warner family's private information was confidential but he could tell Shurman a small amount of information.

Jane and her brother will inherit a huge amount of real estate, insurance money and cash in several banks. Jane had offered to help with all of Billy's expenses you will endure, the lawyer told Shurman. Any doctor bills, dentist bills and school expenses.

After talking to the lawyer, Shurman felt Jane would not take Billy from us ever again. The conversation continued by the lawyer saying, "Jane and her brother's plan is to return to France and live in their parents' mansion. They will go back to school and be cared for in the mansion by the cook and butler who remains living there."

Chapter 29

Our life was starting to look like what every couple dreams their life to be. Having someone you love very much. Having someone you can talk to and know it will be kept private. Having someone who does not criticize or complain if what you do is not perfect or if the house is not always ready for company. And a houseful of children.

We found ourselves in a routine of family first and that is all we ever wanted.

The End

MY LOVER'S BETRAYAL

by Phyllis A. Collmann

Chapter 1

Falling in love was the easy part. Getting to know every detail about someone can be the hard part. We always want to look better than we really are. We are ashamed to tell the bad parts. So, we tell only the good parts of our life.

My life was flashing rapidly in front of me. I had been dating this lovely lady for two months, and it had been going so well.

We both had jobs we liked and worked hard doing the best we could. I worked at my own business of construction, and Julianne worked in a lawyer's office. Our evenings were spent cooking our own meals and having a glass of wine after each meal. It was the best relationship I had ever had.

I started thinking of her when I woke in the morning and several times a day. I would call her on her lunch break, and just hearing her voice made me happy.

The day I started a new construction project started off with a big problem. The problem was the location. The building I was starting on was located in the area where several businessmen wanted a large mall built.

My building was to be a large hotel with a casino and restaurant and an underground garage. I attended all of the meetings the town council requested me to.

Julianne worked for the lawyer that represented

the council. Julianne was always there as his secretary. All I wanted to do was put my arms around her and kiss her like I did at night. I loved just looking at her.

I sat in the audience as a listener, not as the boss of the construction company bidding to build the hotel. Julianne sat down next to her boss, the lawyer for the council. She looked at me, then sat down and slowly lifted her left leg to cross it over her right leg. I could see exactly what she wanted me to see. The picture lingered in my mind all throughout the meeting.

The meeting went on most of the afternoon. I finally was able to leave after the decision was made, not in favor of the councilman representing the businessmen who wanted a mall built. My lawyer came from out of town so I needed to drive him to the airport.

My mind was reeling about the large job and also about the high amount of money I would receive. I was seriously thinking of purchasing a new house I wanted so badly. I wanted to share a new home with Julianne.

I drove home from the airport and found a message from Julianne saying she was tired, maybe we could get together the following night. I texted her and said it would be all right.

The next morning I called all of my workers together for a brief meeting at the site of the new building project. I tried to explain to each one how important this building will be to each one of us.

'The materials will cost millions of dollars. We will be liable for the cost of the materials. We will start as soon as the machines get here to dig the underground garage," I said. "Please make sure you tell your family how many hours you will be working, and how much you love them."

A big roar went up from the crowd of men. I then told them to sign their names for the work. I continued by saying we will be working through the good weather as well as any bad weather.

I said, "If it rains, expect to get wet. If it snows, expect to get cold. You all get paid every two weeks. We start in the morning right at 6:30 a.m. and work until 5:30 p.m. If you put in a couple more hours of work, you will get paid overtime." I finished by saying I would see each one.

My job and the workers were so important to me. If I could help them in their private lives, I was always happy about it. This was a very big job where they could make a lot of money for their families.

The large equipment arrived and began clearing the area and digging the hole for the garage. Some of the materials began piling up. On each pile of supplies, a large brown envelope was attached. I opened the first envelope and after looking at it closely, I took in a deep breath. The prices from the last job had more than doubled. I had to make a quick decision, and the first one was to call my lawyer back again. My second decision was to hire night guards to watch over the materials.

Then I made a call to Julianne. We made small talk about how much I missed her, how much I missed holding her in my arms and how I wanted to kiss her so badly. She suddenly surprised me by asking about the materials for my building, if they had been delivered. I had never lied to her but this meant my getting and saving a lot of money. I lied and said, No. None of the materials arrive until the following week."

Then Julianne asked me if I had started on the project yet. I again lied and answered, "No. The project won't start until next week."

My stomach began to feel nervous. I had to find out why it would interest her. I told her how much I loved her and couldn't wait to see her the following evening. Then I said, "We could have an evening meal at her favorite restaurant, then go back to my apartment. She agreed. I was so in love with her.

I hung up my phone and drove to the site to put canvas over the materials and check on the men I'd hired to guard the materials. The men were so excited to see me. They talked over one another, telling me how a carload of angry men tried to destroy the materials. They helped me cover the lumber with my canvas and the barbed wire. Then they remained guarding the large pile.

Morning came so soon, and I was up and at the site before 6 a.m. I relieved the men and welcomed the other men coming to dig the basement for the garage. It was a very busy day, watching overall the men, then pouring cement toward evening. The crew knew just what they were doing.

I left the men with orders and raced to my apartment to shower and dress in my best. I headed for Julianne's apartment. She was ready and looked so beautiful. I took her in my arms and kissed her like I'd been thinking about all day.

We arrived at the restaurant and were escorted to our table. We sat looking at each other. I loved looking at her. She had long brown hair that curled around her face. Her makeup and lipstick were just right.

The dress she wore fit her body perfectly so everyone was taking a second look. Everything was going so well. The wine was served, and it was delicious just like the meal.

She began questioning me about what I did all day, and if I had started my project. I told her we had a problem with the big digger and hadn't gotten the underground garage dug yet but soon I hoped. Then she asked about the men I had hired. Did I have enough? I told her I couldn't find enough to work the day shift. I couldn't help but notice a small smile on her face. What was going on with her? I needed to find out soon.

The evening was so wonderful. It made me almost forget about her questions. On Sunday afternoon, I made a trip to the site and was so pleased the way everything looked. The guards were ready to go home.

The next group came for their shift.

On Monday morning we poured cement for the hotel's foundation. I arrived in time to see the first cement truck pull into the site.

My trailer was always parked in the middle of the site I was working on. The men were all told they could always come in for coffee or something cold to drink.

I stepped into the trailer, and I was looking at Julianne. Needless to say, the first words out of her mouth were, "You lied to me." She looked so beautiful, yet so fragile.

I opened my mouth and said softly, "I'm so sorry. I just didn't want to talk business with you. I wanted to talk about how much I love you. I want to marry you."

Julianne walked to the door, opened it and walked out.

Chapter 2

That very night one end of our cement foundation was destroyed. It took most of my work crew to repair it so we were now a day behind.

I called Julianne and asked if we could have lunch. She immediately said she was working through her lunch break. I decided to take her a small bouquet of flowers.

I quietly opened the lawyer's office door and walked down the hall to his private office. I reached for the doorknob, turning it very slowly and pushed the door open at the same time. What I saw next made me sick. I wanted to throw up. Julianne was lying on her boss's desk, and he was lying on top of her. My mouth dropped open as my breakfast spilled out over the floor. I ran out with vomit dripping down my shirt.

I started my car and drove to my trailer at the site. I laid down on the bed in the back and cried like a baby. How did I miss her intentions? She did her job for the lawyer so perfectly.

I sat up on the edge of my small bed. I could hear a few of my men talking in the front of the trailer about the amount of money I was spending on the supplies and how someone wanted them destroyed.

Then I suddenly realized someone wanted me stopped and was willing to spend a lot of money to do it. Men were hired. Juliann's lawyer was on the payroll. This meant Julianne had to be getting paid, too.

Going to the police was an option. But, the police and the council worked very closely with each other. My mind was still thinking about Julianne. I could not just stop loving her.

I left the trailer, called out to my foreman and asked for a meeting. I told him to send word the meeting would be at 6:30 a.m. the following morning. At the meeting I told the men we were going to start working around the clock.

"This is important to me, and it's important to each one of you. It's so you will all be safe," I said. I went on to say, "I love my job. So, I do the best work I can, and I hope you feel the same way. You don't have to worry about getting paid. That's all taken care of."

What I didn't tell anyone, including Julianne, is I had made a large investment in the main company that is building this very huge building. It took every penny I had but owning a small percentage of the hotel, casino, restaurant and underground garage would mean a lifelong income for me.

I spent the day hiring additional workers. I explained to each man the new schedule and how the hours were long. The weather may change every day but they needed to be here. I heard a lot of complaining but the pay was so good, most of the men came early and worked hard every day.

I had just gotten to work when my cell phone rang. My heart started beating fast when Julianne asked if she could meet me for lunch. I couldn't say, "Yes," fast enough. We met at a small cafe. At first the conversation was how she was missing me. Then it turned to the construction project. How was it going? How many men did I have working for me? What was I paying each man an hour?

I looked at her and said, "You are so beautiful. I love you so much."

She looked back at me and said, "Oh, I bet your men love you when they get their paychecks."

I finally told her what I paid each man. It was only a short time after that when she said she had to get back to work.

I stood up from the booth waiting for her to stand up. I grabbed her, put my arms around her and kissed her. She gently pushed me away. But, I felt she was surprised I had done that. I was so in love with her. The rest of the day went well. The building was going up with no problems.

The following morning complaints were pouring into me about the number of men missing. I questioned as many of the workers as I could. The story I kept hearing was a man came onto the site and offered them more money. I tried not to think it had to do with Julianne's questions until one of the men told me the man offering the larger amount of money arrived in a large black limousine. I knew immediately who it was and where the money came from. I was not blaming the workers now. I was forced to spend more money on a large fence around the site and hire more men to guard the gate day and night.

I went to bed that night in the back of the trailer. Sleep did not come until nearly morning, and then my phone began to ring.

I answered half asleep. The voice on the other end was hysterical. She was crying and trying to tell me her husband did not come home last night. I tried to calm her down but the more I tried, the louder she got. I asked her to come to the trailer so I could get all of the information in person. I hung up, and the phone rang again. I answered, and it was nearly the same type of phone call. Another man was missing. Now, I was really shaking.

I quickly called a meeting after the breakfast hour. I asked one of the men to write down everything he heard the wives tell me. The wives of the two missing men arrived and told me all they knew and felt. Their stories were almost identical. The night before their husbands had come home from work, then left again to talk to someone who had offered more money.

All my men were confused and angry. I told them the police would be notified immediately but we all had to go back to work. They would work in pairs from now on. I had to get to the bottom of this. I realized it had only been a day that two men were gone but they had never done this before.

The police turned the missing men's file over to a detective to do the investigating. I had a long talk with him about the lawyer Julianne worked for. I did not mention the questions she had asked me. I did not want to involve her. I could not risk hurting her in any way.

The men continued to work around the clock. The third day after no news of the missing men, my phone rang early in the morning with Julianne sobbing on the line. The police were at her apartment wanting to know if she was somehow involved in her boss' scam to shut down my construction business.

Chapter 3

I offered to meet her anywhere she wanted. She agreed to meet at my trailer. She opened the door and flung herself into my arms. This kiss she gave me was the best she had ever given me. She had her arms wrapped tightly around my neck and refused to let me go.

I said, "Tell me what happened."

She said, "The detective caught my boss in several lies. He had tried to blame it all on me because of my relationship with you."

Julianne's voice got very loud. She said, "He ordered me to pick up the two men in the bar and tell them about a new job. Higher pay. Then he ordered me to take the two men to his cabin up in the mountains, north of here. It's an example to the other men when they see me in the bar. They know what will happen to them."

"So now, some are quiting," I said. My voice sounded harsh and angry. I was trying to make her understand how much trouble I'm in because of her boss.

Julianne jumped up from her chair and immediately sat down on my lap. I was really liking it. Oh, how I had wanted her to love me! She put a hand on each side of my face and kissed me. Her body was warm and soft. She felt so good up against me. I wanted her to love me so badly!

I told her she had to tell the detective exactly what

she had told me. She stood up off of my lap. Her eyes vacant and staring through me. She said, "No. I can't do that. If I get fired, I'll never be able to get a job like this one."

"Julianne, your friend is committing a crime," I said.

"But, he paid me for helping him," she said.

I just stood and looked at her. My whole body was in shock.

"Paul," she said. "Please help me."

I told her I would help her if she would do exactly what I asked.

"First, tell me where the cabin is. Do they know your name?" After she told me, I asked her to go home and not talk to anyone.

"Call your office. Tell them you are ill and will not be in for the next couple of days," I said.

Julianne started for the door. Then she stopped, turned around, came back, and laid her head on my shoulder. She lifted her head up, and I looked into her eyes. Her eyes were full of tears falling down her face.

My legs felt like they were not going to hold me up much longer. I slipped my arms around her waist and kissed her. As soon as she closed the trailer door, I sat down and called my foreman. He knew I was serious when he heard the tone of my voice. My instructions were to be followed exactly word for word.

He was to go to the cabin and release the men! He should tell them to go home and come to the trailer in the morning.

The hotel was going up according to schedule. My boss was very pleased. Nothing going on with the workers was reported to him. This was my opportunity, and I was not going to let anyone destroy it.

The two men came to the trailer and told me their story. They were both mad, angry and wanted to hurt the woman that locked them in the cabin. She had told them the huge amount of money they would be getting at this new job. They believed her. Now they wanted to hurt her.

I sat quietly listening to them both. Then I told them it wasn't her they should be mad at. It was the lawyer who was behind the criminal act. After they both calmed down, I told them to go see the detective who was in charge of the investigation and tell him only about the lawyer.

But, I decided at the last minute to tell them I was involved with Julianne, and it wasn't about her but the lawyer she worked for. It got very quiet in the room. The two men looked at each other and then back at me. At that point, I had no idea what they were going to do or say to the detective. All I wanted to do was save Julianne.

When I was alone in the trailer, I called Juianne. She answered after several rings, and her voice was hesitant. When she knew it was me, she sounded relieved. I asked if I could come to her apartment and tell her what I had done.

"Oh, yes!" she said. After being alone all night and all day, she was eager for company. It took half an hour to get there, and my greeting from her was the best I could have asked for. I was going to do everything I could to protect her. I explained several things I thought she should do to be careful. I told her to go to work and not say one thing about the two men locked in the cabin.

"Wait for your boss to say something," I said. "Record all the conversations in the office. Just don't let your boss know it so we can find something to use against him."

Julianne answered saying, "I will do everything you tell me to do."

I left to go to the trailer feeling we were on the exact same page.

The first thing I did when I got to work was check on all of the men and materials being delivered.

The men reported one pile of windows were broken as if someone used a crowbar on them. Also, the lower row of windows in the restaurant facing the street were all broken or cracked.

I went back to the trailer and called the window company. I had to wait until they were finished with another job they were on. Now I have to add a few more weeks to the schedule because of the windows. Also add on more debt.

I backed my pickup to the side of the restaurant and started picking up the broken glass. My foreman came to help. He really looked like he wanted to tell me something. He had heard a lot of gossiping going on among the men, and one thing he heard was a woman was in charge of all the damage being done to the materials and the buildings. I was really nervous over hearing this.

I called the detective, who was working on the case, and asked if he would come to my trailer so we could talk in private. He said it would be late in the afternoon the following day before he could make it.

I made another call to Julianne. She explained to me nothing was mentioned about the new building that day.

Then she said, "I love you." It was the first time she had ever said it. I was extremely happy to hear her say it and offered to come over and bring an evening meal.

She said, "That would be wonderful but I'm very tired and need to get some rest."

I said, "I understand." So we made plans for the weekend.

Nine days had gone by since I viewed Julianne with the lawyer she worked for. I would have handled it differently if I didn't have every minute of my life taken up with my building, men and the debt I'm carrying. But, I truly believed Julianne's boss forced her by threatening to fire her. I knew she loved me.

I arrived at the trailer to find a huge argument going on. The voices were loud, and they all were talking at the same time. I opened the door and stepped in. The first thing I said was, "What the hell is going on?"

The man standing closest to me yelled, "It's all Ted's fault. He fell asleep, and someone sneaked in past him and into the hotel. They spray-painted on all the rooms along one hall. The rooms all have to be repainted."

I tried not to not get angry because I needed every man that was on the payroll. I told Ted to go home and get some rest. Then I told my foreman to tell each man that works a night shift to come in an hour later the following day.

I went up into the hotel and down the hall into the first rooms. It had been painted a beautiful color and now it was spray-painted with black paint. I checked each of the rooms and found I would have to rehire the paint company to come in and repaint all of the rooms, making my debt even higher.

Chapter 4

The week finally came to an end. I went home, showered, shaved, dressed as neatly as I could and drove to Julianne's apartment. She was dressed so lovely in a sleeveless dress. We drove to her favorite restaurant. I walked behind her to our table. I looked down at her arm, and I saw a black spot on the back of her arms. My mind could hardly handle it. I wanted to ask her what it was but I just couldn't do it.

She was being so sweet to me. I didn't want to spoil anything. She asked me several questions about my project but I gave her very little information. That night was wonderful.

The next couple of days went by with no problems. At lunch the second day, I was going into a small cafe. I happened to look in the window, and my heart dropped. Julianne was sitting with the councilman who wanted a mall built on my site. I turned and hurried as fast as I could, practically running back to my trailer. I knew I had to do something but I had no idea what.

Doubt was creeping in. But, I still loved her. If she was in trouble, I needed to know so I could help her. That's when I decided to hire my own detective. I did not have time to take any days off from work and this project. The windows were all replaced. The hotel rooms had all been repainted. We were working on all of the buildings, including the restaurant.

Chapter 5

I had just hung up from talking to the detective, and my phone rang again. It was my boss. He informed me he had purchased four large houses across the street that would need to be torn down and cement poured for a parking area for the casino and restaurant. I sent word to my foreman. He told me the kitchen cupboards were coming that evening for the restaurant. The day was long but I got a lot done. I talked to my foreman and told him to find four men to help unload the kitchen cupboards that night. His response was, "No problem."

At exactly 2:30 a.m., my phone began to ring. I had been sound asleep. It took me a couple of minutes to get a clear mind. I finally said, "Yes," and waited for someone to say something. My foreman's voice was shaking when he said, "The kitchen cupboards caught fire, and they all burned. They are destroyed." Without thinking, I slammed the phone down.

I arrived at the kitchen of the new restaurant in half an hour. I walked in the back door and the smell of smoke hit me. The men were carrying out the burnt cupboards. After they had them all out, my foreman told me how it happened.

"The truck arrived after dark. I had four men unload the cupboard boxes that had contained the cupboards. Suddenly, a very thing young man with his cap pulled down over most of his face started to help. He only carried the small boxes. The boxes were all piled up together. The small boxes were placed on top of the larger boxes. When we were done, we walked out and locked the door and left."

The foreman continued, "When I got home, I remembered I had not seen the young man leave with the rest of us. But was so tired, I laid down on my bed and immediately fell asleep. The fire department called me. The men working in the casino called. Then men working in the hotel called. I was frantic by the time I got there. The cupboards were ashes, and the floor is scorched. We are going to clean it all up. I'm so sorry, Paul."

I opened the door and walked out .I headed for the trailer. I went directly to my desk and opened up my expense sheet. I added on the cost of new kitchen cupboards and flooring to the other damaged materials. Even collecting my paycheck would not be enough to pay for the replaced goods.

I laid my head down. I needed to meet with my lawyer to tell him about this latest loss I'm having to endure. I picked up the phone out of habit and dialed Julianne. She did not answer. Then I called my detective. He was on his way to my trailer. I needed to tell him I wanted him to follow Julianne from morning until night. I finally want to know the truth. My heart is sick and tired of giving her all of my love and doubting her now.

My detective arrived, and it didn't take him long to tell me some news about Julianne. His opinion was he thought she was involved with the man on the city council, not the lawyer she works for.

I asked," How did you find that out?"

He said, "I saw them together a few nights ago, having a meal together and when she left, she kissed him."

He stopped talking and waited for me to say something. It was then I told him I wanted her followed day and night. He was very reluctant but he said he'd do it.

I tried to sleep that night but most of the night, I looked at the ceiling. My mind was on Julianne. I wanted her lips on mine. I wanted her arms around me. I wanted her to tell me she loved me like I loved her.

Chapter 6

Men were working in the hotel, casino and restaurant. They were all told to watch and make sure no damages happened, day or night. The new cupboards for the kitchen were put in. I finally went to the police station and asked if they would drive around the block day and night. I hoped it would scare whoever had done the damage.

The four large houses across the street from the new buildings were being torn down with a wrecking machine. I also had to hire trucks to fill with the old lumber. It was a loud, dusty job.

It wasn't over for me again. Every tire on one of the

big trucks was punctured with a knife. The truck sat flat on the property. No one saw who had done it. No one saw it being done.

I went back to the trailer to enter the expense of the tires in my book. I opened the door and found my detective setting in my chair waiting for me.

The first words out of his mouth were "You're not going to like what I have to tell you."

I said, "Tell me anyway."

He began by saying, "The councilman couldn't get the mall like he wanted so he got his girlfriend to try and break you."

At this point, I asked him to let me sit in my chair. He went on to tell me how she was able to do all of the damages. I listened and sat staring at him.

My mind was so angry. This couldn't be true. But, he went on to say after she damaged something, she stayed overnight with him.

I stood up and said, "You have to catch her doing something. We don't have much time. The houses are nearly down. We have to prepare the ground, then pour the cement. You need to go to the police and report her."

The councilman was so desperate to destroy me. The cement was being poured a section at a time. The first section was nearly dry when Julianne drove an old car onto the cement and she got stuck.

The police caught her running from the car. The councilman had gotten the old car for her.

I did not attend any of the hearings. My foreman was called as a witness as was my detective.

I'm so unhappy and very depressed. I spend as much time as I can by myself. I don't feel like eating anymore. My men either try to help me or they avoid me. They jut can't stand seeing me in such a bad state.

After the trial was over, Julianne only received two years in a woman's prison. She sent word with my foreman, she would like to see me.

The decision to go see her was so difficult for me. I finally decided the only way to get over her was for me to go see her.

I called ahead to the prison office. She was waiting for me in her orange uniform. Not in her usual short skirt and low-cut blouse.

Chapter 7

Julianne wanted to kiss me but she was told, "No touching."

I stood and waited for her to tell me why she did it. The first thing she said was, "I am so sorry."

I answered, saying, "Why are you sorry now?"

"Oh, Paul. I am so very sorry. I was involved with a bad man. He turned on me and blamed me for everything. Now, he is a free man. He told the judge I planned it all."

By the time I left her, I was so confused. Not knowing how to feel.

My foreman walked into the trailer, and when he heard I'd gone to see her, he was in a state of shock. He yelled at me, telling me never go see her again. "Stop seeing her. She will hurt you again."

I had to see her one more time. I didn't call. No one knew I was going. I walked to the door of the area to visit. My surprise could have knocked me to my knees. Julianne was sitting at a table, holding hands with the councilman. I slipped back and out to my car.

My foreman was so right.

I had to put my life back together.

The cement was repaired. The job was complete. I had a large debt to pay. But, I still had a job. I would work through it all.

I would not go to see Julianne ever again.

The End

Being Held Hostage

Chapter 1

I have never loved anyone or anything so much in my life. We met in college. Howard was perfect for me. He was gentle and kind. When we met, he did not rush me. We would meet after each class and walk to our next class together. Having a friend so loyal made the hard classes easier.

We were both determined to do well and graduate. I had had a job in a museum in the city since I was sixteen. My plan was to continue working in the museum. Some day owning it. The owner had told me many times she hoped someday I could buy it from her.

Howard worked in a large bank that dealt with bonds, gold and silver. The company promised to hire Howard full-time when he graduated from college.

Graduation went well. We began to make plans for our future together. Because of our finances, we had a small wedding. We moved into a small apartment. I had never been so happy. We worked so well together. Howard helped me get our evening meals. He helped with the dishes. He helped do the washing. He helped with cleaning over the weekend. Our lovemaking just kept getting better.

I was totally devoted to him. He was open and listened to me each day. He told me everything happening in his office. Love means sharing, and we shared our life together.

Chapter 2

My boss decided to share wonderful pieces of artifacts with other museums in different states. That became my job. I would pack up two or three important, expensive museum pieces and take them in my car and then bring back something we did not have. We would keep them in our museum for a month and then return them. A head of time we advertised each piece.

It was something new for the people in the city to see, and a small charge at the door began to bring more money for the museum. When I traveled to take the pieces and return the pieces, I always got home that night with a nice meal waiting for me. Our love was continually growing.

Howard always showed his love to me by going to the museum the following day to see what I had brought back. He was so supporting.

After we worked and saved, Howard decided to look for a permanent home. Over the weekend we house-hunted with a very professional realtor. It was fun and a joy for both of us. The house we found made us both happy.

The house seemed to fit us both. Howard thought anything we wanted to change or rebuild, he could do it, costing us less money. The excitement of owning our own home made us both so very happy.

Our family was very happy and eager to help us move. It took two weekends, and we were in our new home. It was like a celebration over and over.

When Howard got frustrated over something, he never showed any bad emotions at all. He was calm and quiet.

I was so overjoyed with the way the house looked with all the furniture and decorations up on the walls. We had two big bathrooms on the main floor, one in our bedroom and one for company. We had two complete bedrooms in the basement with a bathroom. Upstairs we had three bedrooms with a large bathroom.

Our family kidded us about all the room we had for a large family. It made me think about it. I felt Howard had to be ready also.

We were finally alone and so very happy. Howard appeared as happy as I was. I hugged him and kissed him because I loved him so much. His lovemaking had changed somewhat. I couldn't say anything because I didn't know if it was me or was it him.

It was a month later he told me his job was going to change a small amount. He was being sent to different banks to deal with their bonds, gold and silver.

I asked him if he thought it would interfere with starting a family. He was very quiet for a few minutes, then said slowly, "No, it shouldn't."

I put my arms around him and kissed him. I wanted to start that very minute but Howard said, "Let's wait until the weekend." Needless to say, it made me feel very uncomfortable.

Chapter 3

Howard came home the next day and said his boss was sending him to a bank a few states away so he would be gone overnight. I stood looking at the man I loved with all my heart. I suddenly found myself doubting him. And I didn't know why. Needless to say, we didn't try to start a family that night.

He was a little cold to me at breakfast but told me he would call me when he got to his motel room. I told him I would love him calling me. I also told him I would miss him very much. He answered saying, "I'll miss me, too."

Howard left, and I sat at the breakfast table and began to cry. I didn't know why except something was terribly wrong. He had never acted like that before. I blamed myself but I didn't know what I had done. He had gone from being so happy with me. So happy with our new home to being and showing he was not happy at home.

I left for work, and the day was long and stressful. I went home to an empty house and tried to sleep that night. The following morning he had not called yet. I was ready to step out the door when the phone rang.

Howard's voice sounded tired as did mine. He mentioned he would be home early. I told him I would bring our evening meal home from work. I told him I loved him.

He didn't answer me. I knew now something was very wrong.

I tried hard that evening to be as pleasant as I could. He mentioned being tired and going to bed early. I kissed him very tenderly when I said goodnight. He went right to sleep.

The days were not as pleasant as they used to be. He came home one evening and informed me the boss was sending him to Europe, and he would be gone all week but home for the weekend. I could not think of one word to say. I was ready to start a family. I needed him here.

He packed all his nicest clothes. Nothing at this point, whatever he said, helped me understand. He kissed my cheek and said, "I will call when I can."

We left the house at the same time. We each crawled into our own car, and he drove away.

My job became more strenuous, and I felt more nervous than ever before. I was losing interest in the museum. My boss realized something was terribly wrong. She thought a day or two off would do me so much good.

I decided she was right. I stayed home the next day. I made a phone call to a friend of mine who worked at the bank Howard did. I asked her if we could meet for lunch. I was surprised she agreed to meet me the next day. I told her how Howard was traveling more away from home.

Gloria was happy to tell me the bank had expanded and was now not only holding bonds but gold and silver. More people were investing. After I left Gloria, I began to wonder if he was just tired. I welcomed him home that weekend by putting my arms around him and showed him how much I missed him. Howard seemed pleased.

By Monday morning our life seemed to be getting back to normal. No one was happier than me. I stayed home again that day. I fixed a nice evening meal. I dressed up, looking my best.

Chapter 4

Everything went very well. Before we prepared for our night's sleep, Howard told me he had to be gone all week again. He was going to a bank in England. Nothing could have disappointed me more. He packed and explained how early his flight was. My world was again feeling like it was falling apart.

He said, "My alarm is set so early. I don't want to wake you," and he went to sleep in the spare bedroom.

Nothing would stop my tears from filling my eyes and running down my cheeks. I had thought of so many things. I thought our life was better, and we could think about starting our family.

We had the house nearly paid for, no outstanding bills at all. We were both driving new cars that were paid for. I was always aware of the amount of money I was spending so Howard could always wear new suits to the bank.

After Howard spent the week in England, he came home late and explained he was not hungry. He took a shower and went into the guest bedroom, got into bed and when I checked on him, he was sound asleep. I crept back down the hall and crawled into our bed and cried myself to sleep.

Howard spent the next week at home, working in the home office. We were pleasant to each other. He came to our bedroom all week. I forced myself on him.

Chapter 5

Howard was home every night for one month, then he said one evening, "I have to go to a bank in South

America for two weeks."

I stood in the kitchen, looking at him in disbelief. He continued to act like it meant nothing but it meant something to me.

He packed enough clothes for two weeks. On Monday morning, he called for a taxi to pick him up. I had offered to drive him to the airport but he refused. He kissed me on the forehead, then picked up his luggage and walked out to this waiting taxi.

I missed work that day because of not feeling good. I couldn't eat anything, my stomach was upset. I blamed it on what I was going through with our marriage. Something was so wrong.

The following day I went to work. The day drug on like it had been doing for a very long time now. I was in the storage room, my mind feeling numb. My boss opened the door and yelled, "Molly you're wanted on the phone."

As I hurried to the phone, all I could think of was how badly I wanted it to be Howard. The man's voice was very stern and serious. He said, "Is this Molly Ebert, Howard Ebert's wife?

How do I describe my body's reaction? "Yes," I answered.

Then he said, "Mrs. Ebert, I am so sorry to tell you your husband has died." From what the doctor told me, it was a heart attack.

Nothing prepares you for a call like this. But I said, "He's in South America."

"Yes, Mrs. Ebert," said the doctor. "We will have to cremate the body and send him home in a sealed box. You can pick out an urn." Then he said, "Do you understand?"

All I could say was, "Yes." I hung up. I told my boss and drove home.

I crawled into my bed with all my clothes and shoes on. I tried to stop my mind from going over and over what the man had said. When I could manage, I called my parents and sister. They were at my house immediately. Nothing made any sense to me. My family all stayed with me that night.

My sister, Terri, moved in with me until the urn arrived. I was having trouble keeping any food down. I blamed it all on Howard's death. When the sealed box arrived, I had it in my arms and kissed it over and over. We chose a blue urn with white doves on it. The memorial was only a blur to me.

My sister took care of everything. She got up the last morning she could stay with me and said firmly, "You are going to the doctor to be checked out."

I dressed and did exactly what she said. It took the doctor only a few minutes to come back in the room with the results. I was two months pregnant. All I could do was cry.

My sister decided I needed her longer. Terri stayed another month until I had Howard's memorial business completed.

Terri left, and I decided I needed to go back to

work. I came home the first day and found a letter from our lawyer waiting for me. I sat down and began to read.

"Mrs. Ebert, this letter is to inform you and explain about your husband's life insurance.

As you well know, your husband's life insurance was taken out for $750,000. But with the cost of hotels, restaurants, rented cars, gas in Europe, England and South America, the amount you will get is $100,000."

I folded up the letter and went to bed.

In the morning, I called my sister, Terri, and read the letter to her. She said in a firm voice, "That can't be right. Why didn't the bank take care of the expenses for him?"

I had no idea. Everything was crashing down on me.

The next day I drove slowly to the bank. Everyone was very nice to me. I went directly into the president's office. He was kind, gentle but very firm. "The bank," he said, "paid all of his expenses."

I sat staring straight ahead. I stood up, and said, "Thank you."

On my way out of the bank, I stopped at the counter and asked about Howard's account. The woman behind the counter had a hard time telling me his account had been closed.

I turned and walked out of the bank. I heard the lady at the counter say, "I'm so sorry." I couldn't answer.

When I got home, I checked his account from his last statement in his desk. It showed, $15,000. Then I added his life insurance, $650,000. He had taken $665,000.

Something flashed in my mind, his new car was not in our garage. He had only purchased it a short time before. I guessed he had sold it.

A few days went by, and I received a letter from the mortgage company. He had borrowed on our house. He had borrowed $200,000 against our nearly-paid-for home.

I now had no choice but to put our house on the market. With the help of my sister, we cleaned it all up so the realtor could show it. I rented an apartment near the museum.

The baby inside me was growing and started moving. Howard was missing out on so much. I did a lot of crying but managed to work each day.

I had gotten into a habit of looking at each man I saw, thinking Howard would walk up to me. That this was only a bad dream.

I missed him so terribly. I thought of him most of each day. I continued to take care of all the business he left undone. The house was on the market. I moved into a small one bedroom apartment. I hoped the house sold for enough to cover what Howard had borrowed against it.

My thoughts of the baby were also on my mind. I needed to purchase a baby crib, all of the baby needs:

clothes, bottles, food. My days were filled each day with thoughts of all that was left for me to do.

The lawyer was keeping me updated. The realtor called me when I had a bid. The lawyer was tracking the insurance money but it had just disappeared. The $100,000 I received from Howard's insurance I put on the money Howard borrowed against the house.

Terri came to my apartment one evening, telling me she was going to South America to the city Howard had worked at while he was there. I explained to her I could only help with a small amount of her expenses. She said she understood. Terri added she believed Howard had done something unlawful.

I found it so very hard to believe. He had always been so honest with me. Now, nothing made sense. I didn't know this person we were talking about. He had always declared how much he loved me until I began to see a change in him.

We had always talked of starting our family. Now it would never happen for us. Only for me.

Terri left, and I felt cold and empty. How could she find something? The memorial was over. The urn was in the cemetery. The tears could not and would not stop.

The realtor called. Her voice was sounding positive about a couple deciding on the house. They asked for two days to make their decision. The financial part of it would clear me from the debt.

I did not hear from Terri until she came to my apartment. When she began to talk about Howard, I had to go to my bedroom and lie down. The baby acted as if he understood what was going on.

"Stella, close your eyes and just listen," Terri said. "I don't want you to have your baby before he's ready. I have a lot to tell you."

Terri began by telling me she had gone to the bank Howard was working in. He has an account with a large amount of money in it.

I lay listening. My thought was why isn't that money deposited in my account back here?

"Stella," she went on to say, "Howard is alive."

I tried to understand what I heard Terri say. Then she repeated it.

"How can that be?" My voice sounded choked up.

"It's true," she said. "I saw him and a very young woman was with him. There's something I had found out at the bank here in town but could not tell you when you found out about Howard dying. Stella, he was with her before he went to South America."

My body was cold. My heart was pounding. I pulled all the covers over my body. I wanted this all to go away. I was so confused. This all had to be a big mistake. How could he do this to me? I had cried at his memorial. I picked out the urn his body was in.

I had been loving him all the time he has been with the other woman. I had been loving him while he made love to her. I have been loving him while he stole all the money from the insurance, also from the house. Howard took from me all of my finances, my pride, my dignity, my trust, all the tender feelings I had for him.

Chapter 6

I stayed in bed over the weekend while Terri took loving care of me. Monday morning my body was able to cope with the horrible change in my life. I went to work.

Terri discussed with me what my life would be like for a while. Then she added, "Stella, we are going to prove him wrong."

I could only deal with one day at a time. So, I tried to eat healthy for my coming baby. I worked hard at work to be able to keep my job. I rested at night.

Terri called me each night after work to see how I was dealing with my life. She said one evening, "When you feel ready, we are going to go after Howard."

My answer was, "Okay."

It was a couple more weeks when Terri called and said, "I'm making a list, and when I have it finished, we are going to sue him for everything he has piled upon you."

Terri's voice sounded excited on the phone. She said she had contacted a lawyer, and he was already to start to work on the lawsuit. Terri's list of financial deception started at the beginning. Howard was paid by the bank but put the debt on my card. He sold his car and kept the money. He took out a mortgage out on our beautiful house. Howard fraudulently took the insurance money by having his girlfriend sign my name on the insurance papers, received the check and then took it with her to South America.

As Terri and the lawyer added it all up, it amounted to over a million dollars. The plan was in the making but it all had to be just right. Terri explained to me the lawyer would make plans to fly to South America and work closely with the bank Howard was working at. The lawyer wanted to make sure the money was in the bank where he could get it so he could get it back to my bank account.

The next few days made Terri and I nervous. Everything had to be a secret. The lawyer went over every detail with Terri. The lawyer wanted all of his expenses taken care of before he made the trip to South America. Terri would take care of it but she expected every penny paid back to her.

I explained to my boss I would need two months off when the baby was born. She readily agreed. The time was getting close. In my state of mind, I didn't remember when the due date was. The store owner I purchased the baby crib from came one evening and put the crib together for me. I had been shopping a little at a time and had all the supplies I needed to start with. My bank account was every low. I had enough to get food and that was all.

I woke during the night, my pains had started. I did not hesitate. I called Terri. Everything was packed and ready. She helped me into the car. It was a long painful process. In mid-morning of the next day, my son was born. He looked just like Howard. The love I felt for my baby was how I dreamed I would feel after seeing him.

Terri and I took my baby home to my apartment. My new life had started. We had not heard from the lawyer. We didn't talk about him. We just took care of my son. My baby clung to my body like his father did when we were first married.

A week had passed, and we had not heard from our lawyer. Terri began to put doubt in my mind. She was now afraid something had gone wrong. She came one evening and told me she had heard from the lawyer. He had reported we needed to keep calm. He was making progress, and that's all he told Terri. He mentioned he had hired a lawyer to help him because he had found how clever Howard was in all his criminal acts of breaking the law.

The first month of my time off had gone by. We had not heard from our lawyer again. Terri continued to check her phone, so afraid she would miss a call from Mr. Brown, our lawyer. We both were getting less sleep each night when we did not hear from him.

Chapter 7

The phone call finally came that we were waiting for.

Mr. Brown said, "We got him. He's in jail. His girlfriend is in custody also." He went on to say, "I'm transferring a large amount of money into Stella's bank account."

I listened to Terri and tried to feel something. I couldn't feel happy because I thought I still loved him. I couldn't feel sad because he deserved his punishment.

When Terri said, "He is to be transported back to this city because he took a huge amount of money from the bank here," I could hardly get my breath. I was sure he would want to see his son.

Terri's advice was "Get yourself ready. Prepare yourself for someone that no longer loves you. You can do this when the time is right."

First, taking my little son into the jail was not what I wanted to do. Second, I really didn't know for sure how I would feel when I saw him. I had loved him so long. I tried to put it all out of my mind.

A few days went by when Terri called me, asking if I had checked my bank account. I had not even thought of it, taking care of a month-old baby took most of my time.

I waited another day. Then called my bank. I already knew what was in my account, very little.

The clerk was attentive until she told me the amount. Her voice changed, was stuttering, but finally told me the amount. I walked to my kitchen chair and immediately sat down. I asked if she would repeat the amount. She tried to do better this time. After I hung up, all I could do was stare at what I had written down on the paper.

Every penny had been taken from Howard and deposited in my account. He had lost everything.

While I was trying to understand and comprehend what was going on and thinking how Howard must be feeling,I heard a loud knock on the door. I was sure it wasn't Terri. She always just walked into my apartment if the door was unlocked.

Mr. Brown, our lawyer, walked in after I opened the door. He started by saying he needed to say this to me personally. Howard is ordering to see his son now.

The shock was unbearable. He had no right to my son after what he did. Mr. Brown explained to me he can see him but he's going to jail. He cannot get his hands on him. He cannot touch him. Let him realize the awful thing he has done.

"Terri and I will go with you," Mr. Brown said, reassuring me. "And, let's do it soon, just to get it over," he added.

Terri came the morning we were to go. Mr. Brown stated he would meet us at the jail. I felt sick all over my body. My son nursed and then went off to sleep.

Terri drove to the police station. We did not talk. I

was holding Colin Ross so tight. He began to squirm so I loosened my hold on him. We arrived at the same time as Mr. Brown. We walked in together. We were led into the jail area.

I could not even begin to describe how I was feeling. My body felt as if it was betraying me. My breath was short and fast. I was panting by the time we got to Howard's cell. Terri stood on one side of me, and Mr. Brown was on my other side.

Howard stood in his cell next to the bars, wanting to see Colin Ross. I knew him well enough. He was trying hard not to cry like I was.

I wanted to say, "How could you?" but I never said a word.

I stood watching him stare at his beautiful son that he will never get to hold, kiss or get to play with.

Mr. Brown said, "Okay. We have to go."

"No," Howard said. "I want to touch him."

"No," I said. "You do not get to touch him." I turned and took a couple of steps. I heard Howard say, "I'm sorry."

I kept walking away and down the hall with my eyes filled with tears.

I had looked into his eyes, and I had seen an older, tired, unhappy Howard. Was he really sorry? Did he regret what he had done? I would never know for sure.

I had spent so many years loving him, planning my future with him, begging to have a family with him.

Now I have to stop loving him, and most of all, stop trusting him, whatever he says.

I had two more weeks before starting back to work. It broke my heart to think of finding a daycare for Colin Ross. The day came, and I prepared to return to work. Terri informed me I did not have to go back to work with money in three banks.

I took Colin Ross with me to the museum to inform my boss I was not returning to work. Telling my boss was so difficult. My boss had news for me. She was retiring, and also selling the museum. With no hesitation, I offered to purchase the museum from her.

My whole life had changed.

The contract was signed, and everyone there continued to work as usual. Terri was so excited about finding me a new home. The house she found was very beautiful and furnished with furniture. I decided it was meant just for Colin Ross and myself.

Chapter 8

I was so busy packing and taking care of Colin Ross. A knock on the door was loud, and the knocking sounded like it was getting louder. I hurried to the door, released the lock, then the door opened.

My breath caught in my throat. I couldn't move. My body was paralyzed. I stood staring at Howard.

This could not be happening but it was.

He looked haggard and smelled bad. Howard spoke first. He said, "I'm out on bail, and I want to see my son."

I opened my mouth. I wanted to scream. He walked around me and headed for the crib.

I took my phone out of my pocket and pushed in Terri's number. Colin Ross began to awake and squirm in his crib. Howard reached down and picked him up. He stood holding him, and I could do nothing but watch. I was so afraid he would try and leave with Colin Ross.

I quickly asked Howard to sit down. I was also afraid he would drop Colin Ross because Colin Ross was very active and it was getting hard to hold him.

When the door opened and Terri walked in, relief rushed through my body. She pulled her chair up close to Howard. She told him Colin Ross needed to be changed, and he gave Colin Ross to her. She handed the baby to me to change him. I needed to feed him also.

After changing the baby, I took him into the bathroom to nurse him. When I came back into the room, Howard wanted to hold him again. Terri and I did not like it but we did not want Colin Ross hurt if Howard made a scene.

We did not like the situation but Terri and I had been told by the lawyer when we had gone to the police station, He had a parental right to hold his child.

My whole body was sick. Everything was finally changing for me. I could feel the love I once had for him leaving. I could see and feel Howard was not the young man I fell in love with. He was not the man I had lived with. He was totally different.

I knew I had to be very patient to protect Colin Ross. My hope was after his trial, he would go to jail and I could raise my son by myself.

Howard stood up and handed Colin Ross to me. He said, "I'll be back tomorrow to hold him." He walked out the door. Terri and I did not say anything to him, fearing what he would do if we said, No," to him.

The decision we made, Terri would stay with me from now on until he ended up in jail. The other decision was we would stay in the apartment. I did not want him to see my new house or where it was located.

My sleep was interrupted most of the night, thinking I heard someone at the door. I was up early to take care of Colin Ross. I nervously went through the morning when I heard a loud knock at the door.

Howard was clean and dressed up. He went right to the crib and picked up Colin Ross. His attitude had not changed. He thought he had a right to my son. Terri was always standing or sitting next to him.

Suddenly Howard stood up with Colin Ross in his arms and said, "I'd like to take the baby to see my family." They lived across town.

I took a couple of steps toward him when Terri said, "I'll go with you." She took the baby out of his arms.

Nothing was going to stop him. I wanted to scream, "No." But, Terri was calm and would keep my baby safe. I knew now what he was capable of doing.

My first thought, his plan was to take Colin Ross to his girlfriend's. If she was here in the city, he would give her Colin Ross to go to South America. Terri would not let Howard do that.

Terri took supplies including two bottles of breast-milk. My head was throbbing. I felt like throwing up. They walked out the door, and I could not stop him from doing this. Howard made it plain, he did not want me to go along.

I quickly called the lawyer. His comment was, "Terri will take care of Colin Ross."

Then I called the police and asked if they would drive around Howard's family home while they were there. I started to tell the police all about him. They stopped me right away. They knew all about him.

Time was going so slow. I was near a panic along with a breakdown when Terri walked in my apartment and handed me a sleeping Colin Ross. There is not a word to describe how I felt. I held my sleeping baby in my arms and swore Howard would never do that to me again.

I sat down in the rocking chair, holding Colin Ross, while Terri told me what I did not want to hear. Howard's family said if I gave all the money back that he had stolen and testified for him, he would only serve one or two years or he could just go free."

I sat staring at Terri until I could answer. I had my answer ready when I could talk. I said, "Howard would take his girlfriend and my son to South America. He is a criminal, and he is going to pay without my money and without my son. I'll testify but it will be definitely against him."

I went on to say, "I am ready to move into my new home. Howard couldn't find us for a couple days until he called my lawyer. Because the lawyer was working for me, he could not tell him.

Howard drove up and down every street and could not find us. The following day was his court hearing, and it did not go well for him. The bank testified against him, along with others. He was found guilty. The ten years he received was not nearly enough.

By the time Colin Ross got to be ten years old, he would have learned his father was not honest. I planned on telling my son exactly what had happened if he asked. If he did not, I would wait until he did.

Yes, his family was disappointed with me for refusing to help him but I was sure Howard would try and take Colin Ross away from me.

The End

Other Books Available

Phyllis Collmann has been writing books since 2002. She has published both a pioneer adventure series as well as several others.

Also Available:

Murder In the Farm Country
Love Gone Wrong
Missing/Trapped In A Blizzard
The Evil That Dwells In The Woods

Printed in the United States of America

About the Author

Phyllis A. Collmann is a retired nurse.
She lives on a farm in northwest Iowa.

In 2002,
Phyllis began putting all of her book ideas down on paper. As the ink from her pen flowed, page after page, her words turned in one book after another.

At age 91,
her retirement hobby is now a work of novel masterpieces.

This book is dedicated to Phyllis' family, especially her husband, Colin. After 72 years and four months together, he journeyed to heaven. Their journey of love has only temporarily paused. For now, Phyllis' journey continues filled with ideas for future books to be penned on paper.